GAME FOR ANYTHING

Also by Bella Andre

GAME FOR ANYTHING

Bella Andre

Pocket   Books

NEW YORK   LONDON   TORONTO   SYDNEY

Pocket Books
A Division of Simon & Schuster, Inc.
1230 Avenue of the Americas
New York, NY 10020

First Pocket Books trade paperback edition July 2008

POCKET and colophon are registered trademarks of Simon & Schuster, Inc.

For information about special discounts for bulk purchases, please contact Simon & Schuster Special Sales at 1-800-456-6798 or business@simonandschuster.com.

Designed by Marie d'Augustine

Manufactured in the United States of America

10   9   8   7   6   5   4   3   2   1

Library of Congress Cataloging-in-Publication Data

Andre, Bella.
    Game for anything / by Bella Andre.
       p. cm.
    ISBN-13: 978-1-4165-5841-5
    ISBN-10:   1-4165-5841-1
 1. Football players—Fiction. 2. Image consultants—Fiction.
 1. Title.
    PS3601.N5495G36 2008
    813'.6—dc22   2007045008

This one's for you, Jessica. Thank you.
And—always—Paul.

ACKNOWLEDGMENTS

First and foremost, I want to thank Gary and Karin Tabke for going above and beyond the call of friendship. Your help was invaluable!

Thank-yous all around for my core group of brainstormers—Jami Alden, Monica McCarty, Barbara Freethy, Anne Mallory, Candice Hern, Carol Grace Culver, Tracy Grant, Penelope Williamson, and Veronica Wolff. I'm blessed by all of your fantastic ideas (even the ones I don't use!) and your endless encouragement. I feel so fortunate to have so many amazing, talented friends.

Thank you, Micki, for making the Bad Boys of Football a very sexy, very fun reality!

Thank you *so* much to my readers. Your support is priceless! I had the best time writing *Game for Anything* and I sincerely hope you enjoy reading it as much as I loved writing it.

And finally, thanks to all of the real Bad Boys of Football for being sinfully sexy and oh-so-bad!

CHAPTER ONE

Julie Spencer could think of a dozen things she would rather be doing than watching the Super Bowl. Even scrubbing the kitchen floor on her hands and knees was starting to sound pretty good. But since her work as an image consultant rarely ended at 5 P.M. even on the weekend, she was sitting next to an important new client at a Super Bowl party, holding a drink she didn't want, feigning interest in a game she didn't like.

If only she didn't have to watch *him* play.

Ty Calhoun was one of the world's greatest quarterbacks. He was also one of the world's biggest jerks.

Even on TV, Ty was too beautiful, too sexy. His chocolate brown eyes smoldered. His biceps beckoned. The slight wave at the end of his midnight black hair enticed a woman to reach out and run her fingers through it to see if it was as soft as it looked.

Thank God the game was almost over. Only eight more seconds, and then she could say her good-byes.

Her client, who had been narrating the game, jabbed her ribs with his elbow to get her attention. "An entire season is hanging on this play. The quarterback has to throw if he wants to win."

Julie nodded politely and focused on the huge plasma TV. All at once the field was a blur of movement. She could barely make out one player from the next.

"The defense is all over his receivers!" Her client was up off the couch, unable to contain his excitement. "If one of those linebackers gets through, it's all over for the Outlaws!"

After what Ty had done to her, he didn't deserve her concern. Still, a foolish part of her wanted him to do the impossible, to make the touchdown and be the hero.

"Oh man, a seam must have opened up! Ty's making a break for the goal line!"

This guy should just relax. Though Ty sucked at relationships, he was brilliant on the football field. He'd pull this play off.

Then an enormous player from the other team hit Ty hard on his right side. His knees buckled, but still, he moved forward. A hundred thousand fans in the stadium were losing their minds, and everyone at her client's party was jumping out of their seats, screaming and cursing at the TV.

Julie fought the urge to cover her eyes as Ty started to fall to the ground. Part of her—a highly irrational piece of her heart—couldn't stand to watch him fail just short of victory.

"He couldn't possibly . . ." whispered her client. "Oh Lord—he is!"

Still holding the ball, Ty thrust it forward with every muscle in his body—and the tip of the ball broke the goal line just as he hit the ground.

Ty Calhoun, the man she'd been stupid enough to give her virginity and her heart to ten years ago, had just won the Super Bowl.

✳

Ty's teammates crushed him between them in a wild group hug, then lifted him onto their shoulders in celebration.

Moments like this were what he lived for. The screaming fans, hot babes whipping off their bras and throwing them onto the field. All his life, Ty had wanted to be a star, a hero. Now, with his first Super Bowl win, he was. And no one could ever take it away from him.

Someone sprayed champagne at him, and as he wiped it out of his eyes with the back of his hand, a flash of blond hair and lush curves in the stands seized his attention.

His heart pounded hard, nearly as fast as it had when he was reaching for the goal line. Was he seeing things? After all these years, had she decided to forgive him?

The woman pushed her hair back from her face and his heart sank. It wasn't Julie. Of course it wasn't. Ty silently cursed himself for being a pathetic idiot.

After all this time, he shouldn't still be thinking about her. About the one incredible night they'd spent together in high school.

Those twelve hours were the only time they'd ever spoken, ever kissed, ever touched. Yet she was still inside his head, and it drove him crazy. All of the supermodels and Playboy Bunnies that had slid in and out of his sheets should have replaced her. And some nights, if their moves were impressive enough, he convinced himself that they had.

But today was different.

Someone poured a fresh bottle of bubbly over his head and he played his part, laughing and high-fiving his coach. He winked at the cameraman, knowing that his face was filling every big screen in the stadium, driving women wild. Was Julie at a Super Bowl party somewhere, celebrating the Outlaws' win? Had she seen his game-winning touchdown? Had she been impressed?

Enough! This was the best day of his life, and he

was going to forget about Julie, soak it up, and let the world worship him.

A reporter shoved a microphone into his face just as security held back a disheveled man who was trying to run onto the field. The man was weeping and looked like he hadn't bathed in a week or changed his clothes in far longer.

The months of rehab Ty had forced his father into over the years hadn't amounted to shit. Ty knew what was coming. What *always* came in moments like these.

"I'm his father!" the man wailed at the guards. "I taught him everything he knows."

No, Ty thought, *I figured out how to be a goddamned football hero in spite of you.*

Fuck the past. He had his friends, endless gorgeous women, and more money than he could spend. He had just won the Super Bowl, and he was going to celebrate.

Whether he felt like it or not.

✳

Five months later, Ty's cell phone woke him up far too early. He ignored it, but whoever was on the other end was relentless, calling back every thirty seconds. He reached out, opened one eye, and looked at the caller ID screen.

Outlaw management. What the hell?

During the off-season, no one interrupted an Outlaw before noon. Certainly not before 8 A.M. These guys paid his bills, but he was the one filling the seats, not some guys in suits. Great players meant great TV, which meant everything to the ad men. The Outlaws' general manager, Sean, should be kissing Ty's ass right now, not pissing him off.

Ty flicked open his phone with one finger. "Ever tried waking a bear during hibernation?"

"We need you to come into the office, Ty."

Ty considered hanging up, but there was no need to be rude. "I'll look forward to seeing you in two weeks, Sean. At training camp. Good-bye."

A thick southern accent came on the line. "You'd better get your ass in here, boy, and quick."

Who the hell was that? *No one* had ever talked to him like that. No one dared.

"And you are?" he asked coldly.

"Bobby Wilson, your new owner. You want to keep your job, you'll be in my office in fifty-six minutes."

Ty hung up and immediately dialed his agent, Jay. He'd made the winning touchdown at the Super Bowl, for fuck's sake! No team owner on earth would talk to his star that way. Not if he knew what was good for him.

Jay told him, "Let's humor the guy. Find out what he's up to."

Fortunately Ty was still feeling good from a big money weekend in Las Vegas, and by the time he'd showered and headed into his living room, he was almost glad he'd gotten up so early. His Seacliff estate had a birds-eye view of blue sky over the Pacific Ocean, the normal Bay Area fog nowhere to be seen. He looked out the floor to ceiling windows to the Farallon Islands and watched surfers ride the waves while kids played on the beach below.

A couple of guys were sitting in his family room banging away on the Xbox, while another was out cold across one of the suede couches.

Ty grabbed a bottle of OJ from the built in Sub-Zero fridge. "Who's winning?"

AJ mumbled something unintelligible, then jammed his thumb into a red button several times in rapid succession.

Ty liked to see his friends having a good time at his house. As a kid he couldn't bring his friends back to the trailer due to his drunk-ass dad, so he'd spent most evenings and weekends at their houses. Their mothers hadn't minded having one more mouth to feed, but he'd often felt like a leech, like he was trying to insinuate himself into everyone else's perfect family.

Now his front door was always open. The party was always on. Even at 8:30 on a fine June morning, three hotties were lying out by his pool, soaking up the rays. Too bad he had a new boss to meet, or he would have joined them.

*

The grandfather clock in Bobby Wilson's office chimed nine o'clock at the precise moment that Ty lowered himself into an oversize leather chair, his agent doing the same. The new head of the Outlaws was on the phone, sitting with his back to the room.

A power play, plain and simple, and not even an original one. It could have gotten Ty's back up if he'd let it, but he'd learned early on that showing emotion put you in the weakest man's shoes.

He'd never seen Sean look nervous before. James, the head offensive coach, looked squeamish too. Neither one would meet his gaze.

Ty already had a list in his head of teams who'd piss themselves at the chance to hire him. Whatever goods the new owner had on Sean and James to make them quiver in their shoes like little girls, the ball was in Ty's corner.

Bobby finally hung up the phone and slowly spun his chair away from the plate glass windows that overlooked the San Francisco Bay. "Here he is, live and in the flesh. The infamous Ty Calhoun."

Ty raised an eyebrow. "Nice to finally meet you."

Bobby Wilson was a textbook bully. Full of bluster, probably because he lacked the goods where it counted.

"You're even prettier in person." Bobby stood up and his thick belly gave way to gravity, falling over his large, shiny belt buckle.

"I had a pretty mother," Ty said, though he wouldn't have recognized her on the street if he saw her. The one picture his father had kept of her was too faded and streaked.

Bobby smiled, revealing teeth that were far too perfect. "I do like to hear a boy speak nice about his mama."

Bile churned in Ty's stomach. Anyone who paid attention to football—or celebrity magazines—knew Ty didn't have a mother. Or a sober father, for that matter.

"I saw you make that winning touchdown," Bobby continued, "and I said to my wife, 'Honey, that boy sure can play football. He knows how to throw that ball and run real fast and get people to buy T-shirts and hot dogs.' The wife likes her diamonds, you know, and she agreed that I should buy the team right then and there. And I was mighty pleased with my new purchase—until I saw your picture in the *Las Vegas Review-Journal* yesterday."

"She was one hot stripper, wasn't she?" Ty said blandly.

Bobby Wilson's face turned almost purple.

"I know you think you can mock me, son, and I know my traditional family values don't mean squat to you, but I will not condone such behavior on any team of mine."

Ty knew the big, rich team owner expected an instant "Yes, sir." All those years of effortless bullying must have made Bobby forget how to work for it.

"You should have seen the ass on her friend," Ty said. "Foxy and Roxy come as a pair, and they're quite a handful—but well worth it."

Bobby didn't need to know that his buddies had wanted to chat up the strippers, not him, and that he couldn't control who took a picture of him with a nearly naked woman on his lap, any more than he could control newspapers printing the shots. It was the price of being a star.

Bobby's eyelids drooped and a sneer slid onto his lips. "I'm afraid I'm speaking a little too quickly for you, pretty boy."

Ty smiled, baring his teeth at the asshole. "The slower the better," he said, mentally ranking the list of teams for Jay to call.

"We're hiring you an image consultant. You have two weeks to clean your act up, or you can get your ass off my team."

Ty laughed. "You actually think I'm going to let some PR person tail me for the next two weeks?"

Bobby looked excessively pleased. "Actually, I

like to think of it as more of a prisoner-warden type relationship."

"If you'll excuse us for a moment, my client and I would like to confer outside," Jay said, intervening before Ty could reply.

Bobby's beady eyes gleamed with malice. "Take all the time you need."

Ty had spent a lifetime facing down opponents who wanted his blood, and was all easy grace and confidence as he left the office. He kept walking out the main doors, down the block to the nearest Starbucks.

"I can't believe I missed my morning coffee for that ass-wipe." Ty didn't like the thought of leaving the Outlaws and San Francisco, but it was the obvious solution to a bad owner who was going to make his life hell.

Jay nodded. "I agree with you, that guy is a major dickhead. He made some money in oil and now he thinks he can take over the hottest team in the league. But just because he's taking a conservative line with his players doesn't mean we should do something rash."

Ty raised an eyebrow. "Rash would be pulling his heart out through his throat."

Jay held up his hand. "Under other circumstances, I'd be first in line to beat the crap out of this guy."

"But?"

"The Outlaws have the best chance I've seen in decades to win back-to-back Super Bowls."

Jay was talking sense. Another Super Bowl would make him a lock for the Hall of Fame.

As if he could sense Ty softening, Jay added, "Plus your friends are all here. I know how you love this city."

Unbidden, the thought *She's still here* popped into Ty's head. He couldn't believe that a woman he hadn't seen in more than a decade actually figured into his plans to leave.

"Besides," Jay continued, "I hear Julie Spencer is the best in the business. I'm thinking it wouldn't be too bad to have her hanging around for a few weeks."

Ty blinked hard. *Julie Spencer?* He knew she was an image consultant, but it had never crossed his mind that they might work together one day.

Jay drooled. "And I hear she's sizzling hot too."

They should be playing hardball with Bobby Wilson right now, but a sudden image of Julie's long, silky legs wrapped around him and her perfect breasts in his hands pushed aside all rational thought.

"Fine. I'll do it," he said, tossing his empty cup into the trash. "But she's the only image consultant I'll work with. If she won't do the job, I'm heading out of town—permanently. Let the Outlaws know for me, will you?"

CHAPTER TWO

J ulie stood on the front steps of her newly pur-
chased office building, feeling proud yet nervous.
As she blew on the steam rising from her nonfat
latte, she gazed at the Bay Bridge, the fishing boats
motoring into their docks, the new mothers pushing
strollers along the Embarcadero, and smiled. She was
going to have to work like hell to make the astronomi-
cal monthly mortgage, but buying the narrow, stone-
faced building along the water had been the right
decision. She felt it down deep in her gut.

She'd just have to be a little less picky about which
clients she took on for a little while, and take on as
much work as she could handle. No big deal. She'd
done it before and she'd do it again.

Julie knew how lucky she was, loving her job so
much. She thrived on the challenges of being an
image consultant; got a huge rush from growing her

company. She'd just hired two more part-time assistants and she planned on being a fixture in the big leagues inside of ten years.

Amy, her soft-spoken best friend from Stanford—and first hire five years ago—poked her head out of the bright red double doors. A feng shui consultant—a gift from her mother—had recommended the color to bring extra business energy to Julie's door. Julie was a sucker for letting her mother feel included in her life, and fortunately she liked red.

"Sorry to bother you before you're even in the door," Amy said, "but I think you should take this call."

"One of our clients?" Julie asked.

"No," Amy said, clearly excited. "Not yet, anyway."

Big clients meant big money! Maybe her financial worries were going to be put to rest.

"The general manager from the Outlaws is holding for you on line one," Amy finished.

Unease shivered through Julie. Even though her office was just blocks from the new stadium beside the Bay, she'd never gone to an Outlaws game. She couldn't—not when her biggest mistake was the team's star quarterback.

The latte curdled in her stomach with a sick premonition. She'd have had to be blind to miss Ty's failures with the media.

Julie stood beneath the safety of her door frame as if taking cover from an earthquake, unable to think, to move.

She could only remember the most important—and disastrous—night of her life.

＊

It was high school graduation night, and Julie's teachers had all congratulated her on being honored as valedictorian. She would be attending Stanford University in the fall; and even though she'd be less than two hours from home, she was excited about the chance to get away, to become someone new.

Somehow she'd made it all the way to eighteen without ever being really kissed. Sure, a drunk guy at a party had once slobbered all over her before she shoved him away, but that didn't count.

No one would believe her if she confessed the truth. Not that she'd do that, of course. What was the point of carefully constructing her image over the past four years if she was going to blow it by announcing to the world that she couldn't attract a guy if her life depended on it?

Especially not a super-hot guy like Ty Calhoun, she thought as she stood on the fringes of the out-of-control graduation party and sipped the slightly sour punch. For four years they'd passed each other in the halls, but she'd never spoken to him. She was in honors classes, while he barely scraped by with tutors. The best high school foot-

ball player in the county, Ty was constantly surrounded by his teammates and cheerleading groupies. His entourage. And she'd bet her trust fund that he'd done it with every one of those girls.

She could hear him laughing as he danced in a circle of fellow students. There was an edge to his laughter that went down her spine and then sat in the pit of her belly. Julie wasn't a social outcast, but she'd never been comfortable at wild parties, never had a taste for alcohol, never been tempted by pot or cigarettes.

She didn't intend to lose hold of the control that she'd built her life around. If her tongue grew loose from booze or drugs, who knew what she'd say? What she'd admit to? Too quickly, the house of cards that was her life could come crumbling down, and everything would be ruined.

Still, she was impossibly, horribly tempted by Ty, a bad boy with a capital B.

Fortunately, the sinful temptation that Ty embodied was way out of her league. If there was such a thing as a babe magnet, Ty fit the bill. No high school boy should be that tall, have shoulders that broad, or dark eyes so wicked.

But she wasn't going to spend her last night in high school drooling at some guy from the sidelines, watching with senseless longing as Ty did the bump and grind with some slutty classmates. It was too pathetic. She found the nearest exit and pushed through it.

Mere seconds after the door shut behind her, she heard it open again. A chill ran up her spine that had nothing to do with the breeze ripping across the Bay. She whirled away from the view of the Golden Gate Bridge. Backing into the deck's metal rail, the bar cold against her overheated skin, she watched the boy she longed for stalk her, slowly, steadily.

She'd fantasized about this moment so many times. The one where Ty finally noticed her, where he asked her to be his girlfriend, where he said he couldn't live without her anymore. She could practically choreograph it.

But now that he was standing in front of her, now that she was looking into his incredible brown eyes, close enough to touch his arm if she wanted to, she didn't know up from down, black from white, could hardly even remember her own name.

"I'm Ty," he said, and she nodded stupidly.

"I know."

His gorgeous lips turned up in a perfect curve. He was even more beautiful up close, like some Greek god come to life.

"You're Julie," he said and she said, "I know," again, sounding like a complete moron.

"Do you know what I want to do, Julie?" he asked, and she could only stare at him. Her lips parted slightly as she held her breath, waiting to hear what he was going to say. His eyes held her captive and her longing was just short of desperation.

"I want to kiss you." His voice fell to a whisper. "Actually, I want you to kiss me."

She blinked at him, suddenly afraid. She didn't know how to kiss. What if he laughed at her? She'd die if he laughed at her.

"Don't you want to kiss me, Julie?"

His voice was silky and hot and she forgot everything except how badly she wanted him.

"Yes," she said. "I do."

"Good."

That one short word rocked through her with its intensity. He said it again, "Good," and something hot settled in between her thighs. She wanted him more than she'd ever wanted anything her entire life.

She moved closer to the boy she had a crush on and went up onto her tippy toes to get closer to his sinfully perfect mouth. He tilted his face down and she reached one hand up to caress his beautiful, angular jaw, running her thumb over his cheek, touching the light shadow of hair dusting his chin.

She was so overwhelmed by just the merest touch of skin on skin that she forgot she was supposed to press her lips to his.

It was a good thing that Ty was no stranger to lust, because he didn't wait for her to come out of her trance. Instead, he went about taking what he wanted—and she loved that she was what he wanted.

He turned his face into her hand, his lips brushing against the sensitive skin, and she shivered at the delicious sensations running through her. She wanted to touch his full, perfect mouth with hers, and her need was raw and desperate as she found him with her lips. With her tongue.

He tasted like wild summer nights, a hint of some unidentifiable alcohol, and passion.

Intense pleasure roared through her as they kissed, his tongue finding a sensitive spot in the corner of her lips. Pushing closer, she instinctively rocked her hips into him, his erection cradled against her belly.

"Enough messing around," he growled, taking her mouth rough and hard. The more he gave her, the more she wanted. She laid her tongue and teeth and hands into him with a fury that matched his. He lifted her up in his arms, wrapping her legs around him, and even though anyone could walk outside and see them, Julie gave herself up to heaven.

Ty's tongue danced with hers, finding more sensitive spots that Julie hadn't known existed. She cupped his jaw again to give herself better access to his delicious mouth. And then her hands were ripping at his shirt and it was falling open.

"I've got the keys to a boat."

"Let's go."

Slowly, he released her from his arms, her soft contours pressing against his hard muscles. He reached for her hand and she could have sworn they were flying down the dock to the marina. Everything felt so surreal, so perfect and magical.

They boarded a huge yacht and his large hands circled her waist in her pink strapless party dress.

"God, you look good," he said as he picked her up
and carried her down the short hallway to the stateroom.
He kicked open the door and a huge king-size bed dared
her to look away. But she wasn't going to back down from
what she wanted. Not tonight. She kicked off her heels
and let him lay her back on the bed, let him look at her
like she was the most beautiful thing he'd ever seen.

Sweet Lord, his chest was a masterpiece. Her fingers
ran across his bronzed skin, and when her mouth grew
jealous she ran her tongue along his pecs, over his nipples, which hardened beneath her lips. He groaned and
threaded his hands through her hair just as she brought
her teeth down on him. She slid her hands down the back
of his shirt, pushing it off his broad shoulders, and then
he was kissing her eyelids and her chin and biting her
earlobe.

In seconds his shirt and pants were on the floor, even
though he never once stopped kissing her. Wearing only
his boxers, his bare leg hot against hers, he hooked his
thumbs under the bodice of her strapless dress.

And then—could this really be happening to her?—
his mouth was on her nipple, hot and wet. Sweet Lord,
how could she have lived for so long without feeling
this?

She pressed her hips into his thighs, and wetness
seeped through her panties, through her thin dress.

Somehow she wasn't embarrassed; being with Ty was the most natural thing in the world.

He slid her dress off, past her hips, and his hand moved to the concave lines of her stomach. He toyed with the elastic edge of her panties and her thighs spread in a clear invitation for him to take any—and every—thing he wanted.

His warm hand moved down, past her pubic bone. Slowly he ran one finger, then two, over her most private, secret spot. She'd touched herself before, but it had never felt like this. Never felt like her entire world was turning inside out, like blue was green, and yellow was red. He sucked her moan of ecstasy into his throat, sliding his fingers down farther, farther still, finally slipping one inside her.

His touch was a sensual invasion of every wall that Julie had ever built around herself, her body, her heart. She wanted him inside of her then, no more foreplay.

More than anything, she wanted him to love her as much as she had always loved him from afar.

"Please," she begged.

But instead of taking her right then and there, he moved his mouth along the same path as his hand, kissing her on her belly and the lacy edge of her panties.

"Please," she whispered again, wanting him to know that she couldn't stand it anymore. She bit her lip hard enough to draw blood and still she could barely keep a scream of erotic frustration from pouring up from her

throat. At the final moment, when she'd given patience all that she had, he slid the lace away from her mound and covered her with his mouth.

She cried out then, a long, low sound. Julie had no defenses anymore. Not from the way his tongue circled her clitoris. Not from the way his finger moved in and out of her. She could go insane from the rush of pleasure taking her over, body and soul. She would have promised him anything just then; all he had to do was ask. But thankfully he wasn't talking, he was sucking and licking and kissing between her legs.

Her hips bucked up off the bed, and as she exploded against his teeth and tongue, she moaned, "Ty!" And just as she found herself wishing that his mouth was on hers, that she could taste him again, he was taking her lips in a kiss that said she was his. Forever.

He slipped a condom on and then the thick head of his penis pushed at her wetness, where his finger and tongue had been.

She wanted to touch him, wanted to feel if his shaft was as hard—as hot—as she thought it would be. Everything about Ty was made to drive her crazy.

"Please," she said again, "I want to touch you. I want to taste you like you tasted me."

He groaned and took her lips again, pushing his thighs between her legs.

"I need to be inside you. Now."

And she was ready for him, desperate to take him

inside. With a groan that was half pain, half pleasure, Ty pressed the head of his penis against her.

"Are you sure you're going to fit?" she asked.

He just said, "Perfectly," as he pushed fully into her in the next breath. He stretched her wide and it hurt so much, but then, it didn't anymore.

Sex was wonderful.

Their hips moved together and even as he grew impossibly huger inside of her, the ecstasy that she'd felt only minutes before welled up again at the base of her belly. He plunged in then out, fast then slow, and with every stroke, with every kiss, she met him with a passion that was as big, as powerful.

He stilled above her, his muscles tight beneath her fingertips. He was going to explode inside of her, just as she had when his mouth was on her. It was all she needed to send her back up to the peak of ecstasy again.

Nothing in her life had ever been this good.

$*$

God, she'd been such an idiot. All she wanted was to forget the day she'd met Ty Calhoun. She wasn't a green girl anymore, not the kind of woman who could be sucked in by a hot jock's charisma and perfect physique ever again.

Julie *never* worked with sports organizations. She didn't trust professional athletes, so how could she get other people to trust them?

She'd simply refer the Outlaws to one of her competitors, who would be more than happy for the ongoing business. After all, athletes were always getting in trouble and their teams were always paying someone to "reform" them in front of the public.

And Julie would try not to mourn the money she was flushing down the drain.

Her stomach churned as she slid on her headset and said hello.

"Sean McGuire here, with the Outlaws. Our team needs to hire a great image consultant for Ty Calhoun, and we think you're it."

She swallowed her gasp and told him she didn't have the resources to take them on as a client, then referred him to another company.

"We'll double your fee. Triple it."

Triple? Sweet Lord! If she took this gig with the Outlaws her financial fears would be a distant memory.

As if he could sense her wavering, Sean said, "All I'm asking is that you come in for a meeting before you say no. We need you."

Had a Crazy switch been turned on in her head? Was she really going to turn down this huge fee, especially since this job could springboard into other big clients?

Yet even if she didn't have a personal history with Ty, how could anyone expect her to change him from a playboy into a solid, reliable man? It was too big a job for one person. And how embarrassing and unprofessional would it be if they found out she'd been one of his early groupies? Especially one who only lasted one night?

"Look," Sean said into the weighted silence, "Ty Calhoun needs you. Desperately. I'm begging you, here."

All the air went out of her lungs. Ty *needed* her? Well, he'd acted like he needed her once before, and she'd been so blind with lust and what she'd thought was love that she'd needed *him* too.

What a huge, enormous mistake that had been.

Nothing was ever going to make Ty change his ways. From everything she'd heard, he was just as selfish, just as screwed up, and just as much of a womanizing bastard as he'd been in high school. Oh, she understood that women wanted to save Ty, and his bad boy antics made him more attractive, more dangerous, more in need of saving than ever.

But she didn't have the *slightest* desire to reform a bad boy. She liked her men intelligent, well groomed, and low-key.

Unfortunately, Sean took her silence as acquiescence, because he said, "We'll be by your office in twenty minutes," then hung up.

Julie blinked at the telephone for a long, confused moment, then ripped off her headset and threw it down onto her glass-topped desk.

"Amy," she called, "I need you to take a meeting for me." But when she poked her head into her friend's office, it was empty.

"Amy just left for a doctor's appointment," her new receptionist said with a helpful smile.

"Oh, right, thanks," Julie said, hating the way she was stumbling over her thoughts—something she never, ever did.

Pull yourself together. This meeting would be no different from any other difficult situation. She'd be cool, composed, and unflappable. No matter what Ty said or did, she'd refuse to be baited. She felt nothing but pity for the man he'd become. A boy could be excused for his actions, but a man had to take responsibility for his life. Based on media accounts of his wild partying and speeding tickets and evenings with strippers, Ty was as far from responsible as a person could be. No matter how good he looked when he walked in the door, pity would be her only emotion.

As she redid her makeup, made sure that her fishnets didn't have a run, and buffed her peep-toe, black patent leather heels, Julie reminded herself that anything she'd felt for him had died long ago.

And nothing could ever bring those pointless feelings back.

CHAPTER THREE

Ty followed Sean through a shiny red door into Julie's office, and didn't even stare at the cute receptionist's nicely showcased ass. Not today.

Today was all about Julie.

He looked into the glass-walled offices beyond, not surprised to see that Julie had done very well for herself. She'd always been poised to be successful, to take what she wanted.

And then he saw her, pushing open the door of her office, walking straight toward them. A surge of emotions shot through him—longing, hope, pain, lust—and he knew the only way he could deal was to shut them all down.

Heat shot straight to his groin. Even in her buttoned-up-to-the-neck sweater and knee-length skirt, Julie put every other woman he'd been with to shame. She was still the bar by which he measured the female sex, and everyone else came up short. Way short.

Her legs seemed to go all the way to her neck, and they were neither pencil thin nor overly muscular. She had rounded calves that he wanted to sink his teeth into, the sexiest kneecaps he'd ever seen, and her thighs would tempt a monk. Plus, that glorious ass of hers created the perfect waist-to-hips ratio. They were the perfect handful for grabbing onto when she was riding above—or below—him in bed.

Ty's gaze moved past her waist and up to her chest. Damn, a guy could be moved to write poetry about breasts like those. Marilyn Monroe would have had some stiff competition if Julie had been around in the fifties.

Finally raising his gaze to her face, he took in the ice-cold eyes that studied him as if he were a bug beneath a microscope.

One that she wanted to spear beneath her very sexy stiletto heel.

Okay, so she was still pissed at him. No big surprise there. A flash of guilt hit him square in the chest, and he couldn't believe he was still feeling bad about things after all these years.

Grad night had been the usual party mix of drinking, dancing, and sex. The only surprising thing was that the sex had been with a virgin.

With Little Miss Perfect.

With the one girl he'd always wanted but knew he could never have.

He'd never been good enough for her, and one look now at her expression told him that all the money and fame and success in the world hadn't changed anything.

＊

Julie seethed as Ty reached out to shake her hand. How dare he walk into her office as if he'd never ripped her heart out of her chest and thrown it overboard? Her final words to him on the morning after grad night played over and over in her head.

I hate you. I'll always hate you. And I never, ever want to see you again.

After ten long years, she hadn't been able to think of anything more sophisticated and cutting that she could have said. Not when her heart had been broken into a million, billion pieces. Not when he'd stolen her virginity and then dumped her in the most humiliating way possible less than twenty-four hours later. The bastard.

In the back of Julie's head a voice whispered, *Are you sure he really stole it from you? Didn't you practically shove it at him like the desperate virgin you were?*

As far as she was concerned, that voice—and Ty—could go to hell.

Forcing herself to shake his hand in as detached

a manner as was humanly possible, Julie acknowl-
edged another big reason for her anger: Even after a
lifetime of hard living, even though he rated a negative number on the scale of humanity, Ty Calhoun
was still the most incredibly gorgeous man she'd
ever set eyes on.

He'd been a hot, hunky teenager. And now, ten
years later, he had the build of a warrior. Beneath his
expensive shirt and overpriced jeans, his well-trained
muscles were hard and tight. His jaw had filled out
just enough to lend a rough edge to his male beauty,
and the light stubble that covered his chin drew her
attention to his lips, which held incredible sensual
promise.

"Nice to meet you," she lied, hating his smirk,
hating the fact that her body still responded traitor-
ously to his touch. Goddamnit!

Julie pulled her hand away, reminding herself
that she was in complete control of the situation.

"Now, Julie," he drawled, "I can't believe you
don't remember me."

She itched to smack the lazy grin off his perfect
face even as she searched his eyes for any sign of
remorse. Nothing. Just as she'd figured:

Once an asshole, always an asshole.

Raising a condescending eyebrow, she tilted her
chin the slightest bit as if she was trying to place

him among her enormous list of other unimportant acquaintances.

"Oh yes, now I remember you," she said, pleased with how smooth she sounded. "Didn't you go to my high school?"

"Sure did," he replied, and she could feel him laughing at her with his eyes, practically hear him thinking how pathetic she still was after all these years, trying to pretend that she didn't know him. He probably thought she had run home to dress up for him, that she was wearing sexy heels and fishnets to try and seduce him.

Sean studied the two of them between narrowed eyes. "You two know each other?"

"Yup," Ty said just as Julie muttered, "Barely."

"We ran in different crowds," Ty clarified. "She was class president, went to Stanford. One of those brainy, do-good types."

"And he was a jock," Julie spat.

Sean laughed. "Thank God for that. Jocks pay my salary, you know. But fact is, we need you to make everything nice and pretty for us again. With the media, the fans, and especially the new team owner, who's a full-blown southern conservative."

Julie led the two men to her spacious, colorful office, knowing Ty was taking it all in. *Bet none of your little playthings know how to run their own business, do they?*

Sean didn't waste another second making his sales pitch. "It's pretty obvious that you don't have a very high opinion of jocks. Or Ty."

Julie almost laughed. Talk about being up-front! It was an impressive, and disconcerting, tactic. She nodded. "That's right."

An odd expression flashed across Ty's face, quickly replaced by his I-don't-have-a-care-in-the-world-and-yes-I-was-born-looking-this-good mask.

"Perfect," Sean replied. "You're exactly the right person for the job."

Ty's and Julie's heads jerked toward Sean in surprise.

"Here's how I see it," Sean explained. "Since you don't like football or our star player, you know exactly what other people are having a problem with. You get the issues. Now we just need you to make them go away."

"He parties too hard and sleeps with too many bimbos," Julie stated bluntly. "Dressing him up and having him say a few nice things to the press isn't going to make much of a difference. Not to the public or a new conservative boss."

"Keeping tabs on me, Julie?" Ty asked cockily.

"You're right," Sean said, ignoring Ty. "He's a piece of work. He's also the best thing football has seen in the past decade. We don't want to lose him. *I* don't want to lose him. He's not only the best quarter-back around, but he's my friend. So I'm asking you again, would you please take him on as a client?"

Ty gave Julie a look that said, *See, I'm still the hottest game in town, baby,* and she stifled the urge to throw a heavy glass paperweight at the sexy, egotistical SOB.

"I'm asking you to name your price for two weeks with Ty," Sean continued. "We'll throw in perks, a car, whatever you want, in addition to a super-size fee. We can't change his image and make the big boss happy without you."

She calmly said, "I've already told you that my firm is unavailable at present. I'd be happy to phone several other image consultants while you wait."

"Are you scared of me?"

Ty's words were just to the left of taunting, just to the right of a sexy challenge. Julie felt her lips draw into a tight line; she forcibly relaxed the muscles in her face. Like hell if she was falling for *that* trick again.

"You're not important enough for me to have an opinion of you one way or the other," she said coolly.

Hearing the words come out of her mouth, so strong and confident, Julie even believed them herself.

Which meant . . . she *could* take the job. She knew exactly what he was now so there was no chance he could fool her again.

So in return for a bigger paycheck than she thought she'd ever see, she'd spend two weeks with a man to whom she'd been just a teeny, tiny notch on a very long belt—and this time, she'd walk away laughing.

CHAPTER FOUR

What have I done? I'm in big trouble! The thoughts whirled around in Julie's head as she followed Ty's flashy Maserati in her economical Prius. She'd nearly called Sean back to tell him she'd made a mistake, that she was the last person on earth to try to set Ty on the straight and narrow, that they needed to find another image consultant, any other one but her!

How was she going to make it through the next two weeks? Even the next hour was worrying, since a familiar warmth had already settled between her thighs and the tips of her breasts felt sensitive as they rubbed against the cups of her lacy bra.

Five minutes in her office with Ty and she'd been reduced to a quivering pile of hormones. And they hadn't even been alone! How on earth was she going to keep it together when it was just the two of them?

How could she possibly keep her panties on around him?

He pulled his senselessly expensive car into one of the slots in a six-car garage of one of the most stunning houses she'd ever set eyes on, and she whispered to herself, "You've got to be kidding me."

Julie had grown up with money. Lots of money. Yet she'd never seen anything quite as impressive as Ty's estate, smack-dab on the water in the Seacliff district of San Francisco. Over the past few decades, houses here were selling for $15 to $20 million, only to be torn down for sprawling McMansions to be built in their place. The glass-and-steel structures often looked out of place in the once architecturally rich neighborhood.

Surprisingly, Ty's house looked to be original—albeit updated—1920's architecture.

Julie would much rather have had their first planning meeting at her office, with her staff nearby to protect her from his charm. A crowded restaurant would have been even better. Anything other than Ty's personal kingdom. But he'd insisted.

"Now that I'm your top client, don't you need to get to know me?" he'd said.

She'd been so upset with his easy maneuvering of her and the situation that her reply had been cutting. "I suppose I do need to see everything that's wrong before I can begin to start making changes.

What better place than your house? I'm sure it's a treasure trove of surprises."

Again, pain flashed in his eyes too quickly for him to shutter it. How was he managing to make her feel like the bad guy? He'd been the one who'd hurt her. Not the other way around.

She sat behind the wheel of her car a moment too long and he opened the door for her and held his hand out. She didn't want his help, even if it was a surprisingly gentlemanly thing to be doing.

"Maybe I won't have to teach you absolutely everything about proper behavior," she said as she placed her hand in his in place of a thank-you.

As she stood in his driveway, she felt like she'd lost her entire foundation. She'd never wanted to be this close to Ty again or have him look at her like that—like he wanted her to kiss him, just like he had when they were eighteen and she'd been so delighted by his attention.

And now here they were and it was as if the past ten years had never happened. Because she was still consumed with the same pathetic lust and desperation.

She quickly pulled her hand back and he put his up in a gesture of surrender.

"I know this is a pretty rough surprise, having to work with me. If you'd rather not take me on, Julie, just say the word. I'm sure the team can find someone else to clean up my act."

She stared at him, hearing the challenge beneath his words.

"Oh no, I'm definitely up to the test," she said, suddenly remembering that she was supposed to be the one in control here, not him. Still, as she walked up his beautifully paved driveway, knowing his eyes were trained on the sway of her hips, the curve of her calves in her heels, she gave quiet thanks for the angel that helped her choose one of her sexiest business outfits to wear this morning. Just think if she'd been PMSing and had put on that frumpy brown-pant suit that she'd been meaning to give away for the past few months. God, that would have been embarrassing.

His front door was open and she wondered if he had trained his servants to open the door, put the champagne on ice, and turn down his silk sheets the moment they saw him coming home with a woman.

Julie knew she didn't measure up to the hot babes he normally dated, but some twisted part of her actually hoped that his staff would think that she *could* get Ty, rather than just be a paid business associate.

Nonetheless, she couldn't fail to be impressed by his house and property. The foyer alone had one of the most beautiful views in all of San Francisco. The Golden Gate Bridge glittered red in the sunlight to her right, the surf and the Farallon Islands directly in front of the house.

He'd certainly come a long way. And even though their past was messy she admired all he'd achieved. From life in a trailer park to all this. While she worked for what she had, she'd never had to struggle for money or respect. Not like he had.

A large yacht motored past his house just as she felt him move behind her. Suddenly she was eighteen again, standing at the rail of the marina in Sausalito, knowing the boy she adored was close enough to touch.

"It's beautiful," she said.

"More beautiful than I ever imagined," was his slightly gruff reply near her left ear.

She didn't think he was talking about the view from his house. Julie could feel his breath on her skin, his heat at her back. She wanted nothing more than to turn to him, to give herself up to the incredible pleasure of his touch.

Just when she didn't think she could hold out another second from doing the second stupidest thing in her entire life, shouts rang out from the large room off of the foyer. Taking it as her cue to get away from Ty, she dashed into the impressive kitchen. Just beyond the enormous granite-topped island, she saw three large men in various states of disrepair dancing on colorful plastic floor mats in the family room.

"Dude," one of them said without looking over

his shoulder at Julie and Ty, "I just totally trumped Alex. I told you guys I was a Dance Dance Revolution king!"

Ty grinned and leaned against a sink. "Now that's something to be proud of, my friend."

Ignoring the silly part of her that wanted to kick off her shoes and dance to the music pumping out of Ty's enormous flatscreen TV, she coolly said, "I'd love to meet your friends."

"Guys, this is Julie."

All three men—if you could call shirtless guys who hadn't shaved in well over twenty-four hours playing a kid's video game men—spun around to meet Ty's groupie of the hour.

The Dance King's eyes lit up and he whistled as he looked her up and down and then back up to her breasts. "Well, hello there, pretty lady," he finally said as he managed to tear his gaze away from her chest and make eye contact.

She gave him her primmest smile in return. "It's so nice to meet you."

Ty's incredible estate was nothing more than a glorified frat house. They wouldn't get any work done in this kind of environment. Besides, didn't he care that his friends were eating his food, messing up his house, and playing with his toys, but didn't respect him enough to keep the front door shut or throw away their pizza boxes when they were through?

Without bothering to confer with Ty—after all, he was her client and her word was law from here on out—she walked over to the couch and began picking up shirts and socks and shoes between her thumb and forefinger.

"And who does this belong to?" and "Is this yours?" mingled with the electronic beats playing on the enormous TV.

As the three very confused men dutifully dressed themselves, she found the remote control under a discarded sweatshirt and hit the Power button.

She assumed the guys who now stood before her in wrinkled clothes were also football players. But even though they had bulging muscles and the letter *O* was shaved into the side of one man's head, they seemed no more fearsome than little boys.

"Why don't you head home, take a shower, eat something, and get some rest," she suggested to them.

"Who are you?" asked one man.

She smiled. "Ty and I go way back."

Everyone in the room simultaneously smirked so she said, "He asked me to clean up some messes for him," then looked pointedly at their collective untidiness.

She caught Ty's shrug from the corner of her eye and had to hold back a giggle when the biggest, brawniest, meanest-looking guy said, "I don't know who you're calling a mess, dude, but I'm outta here."

"Me too," said the others, but not before they helped themselves to a couple of sodas and dough- nuts on their way out.

"Close the door behind you, please," she called out, feeling deliciously puritanical.

Unfortunately, Ty knew exactly how to keep her from enjoying her newfound pleasure in kicking butt. "You've got to check out my pool," he said, just as a stunning young woman unfurled herself—all long arms, legs, enormous naked breasts, and tiny waist—from his hot tub. And there wasn't just one Amazon lounging in perfect near-nakedness beside his pool, but two.

Julie knew she was attractive, but in a beauty competition with women like these, she was the sure loser.

Her second thought was even odder. For the first time, it occurred to her that it must be quite a burden on Ty to be so good looking. And so rich and success- ful too. How could he know if any of these people were true friends? If they really liked him, or found his jokes funny?

Incredible. All the bronzed, toned flesh and sili- cone was making her so loopy, she'd actually spent five seconds feeling empathy for a man who had it all.

But why did everything in his life have to be so senselessly over the top? Yes, he was trailer park boy done good, but couldn't he do good for other people as well, rather than just himself and his equally pretty friends?

And then, she smiled. Because she'd just figured out how she was going to reform Ty: not only in the public eye, but for his own good too. He was going to spend the summer doing good things for other people. Even if it went against the natural inclination of every bone in his body.

The first stop on that train was pulling the rest of the leeches off and throwing them back into the water. Bye-bye, girls!

With unmitigated glee, Julie said, "Hi, ladies, I'm the new cruise director. It's nice to meet you."

The topless redhead scrunched her nose. "Um, we're not on a cruise."

Julie didn't laugh; that would be downright cruel. "Nope, just a figure of speech." She clapped her hands together. "In any case, your friend Ty has a lot of important things he needs to take care of, so I'm afraid you'll have to be on your way."

The blonde slipped her sunglasses off. "Anything I can help with?"

Ty smiled at Julie. "Cindy here is real good at following directions."

The fact that fire didn't shoot out of Julie's ears was

a miracle. A vivid image of this girl touching Ty, doing all the things to him that she'd done so many years ago, that she'd helplessly dreamed of doing again and again for a decade, nearly did her in. Julie wanted to take the blonde down, rip the silicone out of her breasts, and make sure she never came within a mile of Ty.

Instead, Julie smiled and said, "Don't worry. I'll give you a call if we need you for anything." *Like when he needs his toilet cleaned.*

Surreptitiously, she watched Ty to see if he was drooling as the girls put their very skimpy clothes back on. Strangely, he didn't seem to be all that interested in the show they were putting on for him. Instead he pulled out his BlackBerry and checked his email, typing in a quick message. Even when each girl pressed against his arm and gave him a peck on the cheek, he barely looked up.

She'd never met anyone who appreciated a woman's curves as thoroughly as he did, so what could be the explanation for his diffidence with these women? What man on earth wouldn't be dying to have immediate sex with them?

Ty slipped his BlackBerry into his back pocket and grinned at her. "Good work. I couldn't have cleared the place better myself."

She frowned. He wasn't supposed to be happy with her kicking his friends out. She'd been trying to get under his skin, piss him off a little.

And he definitely wasn't supposed to focus his attention on her and say, "Looks like it's just the two of us now."

What have I done? It was her own damn fault for thinking she was smarter than Ty. Or that she had a prayer of a chance of resisting him.

CHAPTER FIVE

I t was a turn-on to watch Julie be such a ballbuster, even though he was pretty sure that wasn't the intended effect. He knew she wanted him to think she was in charge of the game, and he was perfectly happy to let her act like she was leading him around on a short chain.

But he was glad she'd kicked his friends out of his house. Sure, he enjoyed the constant party, the sense that he lived in a resort with bikini-clad girls by the pool and an endless supply of good food and drink at hand. But sometimes it did get a little old.

Sometimes he wanted to be alone for a little while. To turn off his smile, drop the banter, escape the pressure to be playful and sexy with the ladies.

If he were a nice guy, he'd tell Julie that he hadn't slept with Cindy or her friend. But he liked seeing Julie jealous. Even more, he enjoyed watching her work to tamp it down, to pretend that she didn't care who he slept with or how big the woman's breasts were.

Oh yes, Julie cared. And Ty was extremely glad that she did.

He hadn't spent a lot of time feeling bad about himself or wishing he could be a different person. He'd grown immune to insults long ago. Growing up with a drunk in the house did that to a guy. But somehow, when she said he was worthless, it kind of grated. Just enough that he noticed.

Sure, she was only a youthful infatuation made more important by the fact that he hadn't seen her again after their one rocking night together. But he still wanted to impress her. And not just with his car and his house and his bank account. That wasn't enough.

He was going to take her into his private sanctum beneath his house.

No one, except the men who'd built it, had ever been below his garage. Ty had designed and furnished the space himself, to suit his needs on the days when he wasn't up for the party.

"So," she said, "where should we sit down to start ironing out your new schedule? We'll need to get your agent on the line, as well."

She was eyeing the large dining table, probably hoping she could sit at one end while he sat at the other.

Not a chance.

"I've got the perfect spot." He nearly laughed when she narrowed her eyes in suspicion. She always was a sharp one, and a babe with brains was a helluva combination.

"Follow me."

They wound through the house and into his spacious garage. He touched a button on the wall and a five-foot section of the floor slid open to reveal a marble staircase.

"Are you kidding?" she said, backing away in horror. "I'm not going to follow you down there."

He laughed. "What do you think I'm going to do? Cut you up and store you in my freezer?"

"Of course not. But—"

Her cheeks grew pink and Ty filled in the blanks himself in his head. *But you might kiss me and I might like it. And then we might end up with our clothes off. Again.*

At some point they needed to have a discussion about their past. Big stuff had gone down and it couldn't be ignored forever. But it was too soon.

She was like a skittish horse, always on the verge of running. Fortunately, Ty was more than willing to be the Julie whisperer.

*

To say that she was nervous as she walked down the long flight of dimly lit stairs was an understatement. What if Ty was some kind of freak like Picasso and had filled the walls with all sorts of S and M pictures? What if he had S and M equipment down there? Julie wasn't sure what that entailed, but she was guessing that whips and chains and leather clothing with holes cut out in various places weren't too far off the mark.

She shivered. She should be horrified at the thought of Ty being into S and M. So why was she helplessly titillated by the thought of putting leather on for him? Of being tied to a bedpost while he watched?

Ty flicked the lights on, and Julie gasped in shock.

Warm, dark wood shelves surrounded the room and the thick leather-bound volumes seemed to be well-worn, their spines creased as if they'd been read time and time again. The walls held stunning artwork by Impressionist masters—Matisse, Degas, Renoir. She knew the difference between a print and an original canvas, and Ty's paintings were the real thing. She couldn't contain her wonder.

"Is that really a Rodin?"

He nodded and she somehow managed to pull her eyes away from the stunning treasures to look at

Ty. No one had ever surprised her so much before. She didn't know what to think, what to say.

"This sculpture is my most prized possession," he said, reverently running his fingertips over one ballet slipper of the two-foot-tall bronze sculpture of a ballerina.

Where Julie had expected to see smug satisfaction was something else entirely: awe.

Her traitorous heart leaped within her chest and it took everything Julie had to quell the beast inside her that wanted to love Ty again.

No, no, no!

Just because she was impressed with the things he possessed didn't mean she was impressed with him. How could he have possibly collected so many amazing things? Or had a designer told him that great artwork would impress his guests?

She shook her head. If that had been the case, he wouldn't have so many amazing modern works in the large room as well. His den bore the stamp of a man who knew exactly what he liked.

She didn't like feeling as if she'd just found a piece that couldn't possibly fit the puzzle she had already completed. She didn't like to think that Ty could have another side or, God forbid, depth.

She moved through the room, lingering over the books, the paintings, the other sculptures.

"Aren't you afraid your friends will ruin these

during one of your parties?" She winced at her tone. She hadn't meant to sound so uptight, so prissy, but Ty had been throwing her off balance all day. "What I mean is, everything in here is priceless. Amazing. I'd want to keep it all to myself."

He remained standing in front of the Rodin. She was dying to look at the beautiful piece up close, which meant she had to stand next to him—a highly inadvisable move.

Ty waited to respond until she was merely inches away. "My friends have never been down here. No one else has ever been down here."

She frowned. "What are you talking about? You brought me."

He smiled, and her breath whooshed right out of her body.

"I know," he said, and she swore to God that her knees went weak. Pathetic.

She took a step back and then another, until she backed up into the lushest, softest crimson sofa in all creation. Even the furniture in this room beckoned to her, which was saying something, considering she'd always liked clean, contemporary lines. She sat down and closed her eyes in appreciation. No seat had ever felt this good, had ever cradled her better.

Lord, things were far worse than she'd thought— she wasn't just falling for his art, she was getting a thing for his couch too!

"Comfortable, isn't it?" he asked, leaning against the bookshelves, his muscular, tanned arms crossed across his chest.

He looked like a lion in the heart of his lair, surveying all that was his with deep, unmitigated pleasure. Would he stroke her as reverently as he had the Rodin? Would he look at her with the same kind of wonder that he did his Monet?

Thankfully, the voice of self-preservation told her to reach into her briefcase for her "serious businesswoman" glasses so that they could work up the plan for his image reversal.

Thereby getting her the hell out of his house in one piece.

Preferably with all of her clothes intact.

"Okay, then, why don't we get down to business?"

"With pleasure," he agreed. Though he sat on the facing couch and kicked his long legs up on the antique coffee table, she didn't trust him.

Not when the word "pleasure" sounded like a clear and direct invitation to sin.

She pulled out a file of newspaper and magazine clippings. "Sean gave me this and said it would help me get a handle on your image thus far." She pulled out a particularly indicting photo of him locking lips with a mostly undressed brunette. "Impressive stuff."

He grinned. "You're right. The doctor who created those breasts was an artist."

She almost laughed, but she needed to straighten him up, not encourage him to be a jokester.

"My job is to stop photos like this from being printed. Do you know what the first step to that is?"

"Pay off the editors?"

"Don't be a smart-ass."

"Then don't ask dumb questions."

She sucked in a breath.

He took advantage of her momentary silence and moved to sit next to her. "Look, sweetheart," he said and she hated how much she liked it when he used an endearment, especially given that he'd just insulted her. "Neither of us are idiots."

She pressed her lips together and tried to stop looking at his mouth, but his eyes weren't any better than his beautiful lips.

"Don't call me sweetheart," she said in a no-nonsense tone, though she sensed that he knew he had her right where he wanted her. The lion hovered over his prey.

Suddenly everything shifted as he relaxed back into the couch.

"I shouldn't be messing with you," he said, "and I apologize for that 'dumb' comment. It's just that I've spent most of my life being treated like a brainless jock. It gets pretty old after a while."

Not only was Julie immediately chastened by what he said, but she felt like a complete and utter idiot. He hadn't been coming on to her. She was nothing special to him.

He was just *"messing with her."*

She should be celebrating the fact that she was going to make it out of his underground lair free and clear with all of her clothes intact, after all. So why wasn't she happier about it?

Why did she feel like crying?

"And I apologize for the 'smart-ass' comment," she forced out. Trying to get back on track, she said, "I think the best thing for your image would be a series of charity events throughout the Bay Area."

"As long as they don't interfere with football camp next week."

"Sounds to me like you won't make it to camp if you don't take care of this," she pointed out.

Something flashed in Ty's eyes and in an instant he was the predator again. "Have you ever been wrong about anything?"

"Excuse me?" she asked.

He moved closer. "I think my question was pretty clear."

She swallowed, tried to lick her lips. "Rarely."

"Okay, then. How about surprised?"

He'd just surprised her by bringing her to his private sanctuary, and she'd been surprised by how strongly her body reacted to his nearness after all these years.

"No," she said, but her voice was weaker.

His smile was wicked this time. "Good thing there's a first time for everything."

She should move to the other end of the couch, or better yet, run up the stairs and out the door. Anything to get away from the sensual pull he held over her.

"I've been surprised before," Ty said, not seeming to expect a response—which was good, since she wasn't capable of giving one at the moment. She was too busy trying to remember how to breathe, how to keep her head on straight, how not to dive at his mouth and tear all his clothes off and beg him to take her right this goddamned second!

He leaned down and said, "Don't you wonder what I was surprised by, Julie?"

"No." But what she meant was, "Yes, oh yes!"

He brushed one finger against her cheek and said, "You."

She was so caught up in his touch, in the way he was looking at her like she was everything he ever wanted, that she forgot about running. Forgot that she hated him. That he was only equipped to hurt her, no matter how good he was capable of making her feel.

Her silence amused him, she could tell by that lazy grin, the way his fingers moved across her lips. She felt funny all over, like she'd left her real body, her brain elsewhere.

"Don't you want to know why?" he asked.

Desperately.

But she couldn't admit that. Not even now that she'd almost given herself to him by not pushing away his hand, by not reading him the riot act for slamming through the client-consultant boundary. If she spoke she'd only betray herself, her longing. She tried to shake her head no, but all her small movement did was cause his fingers to slide all the way across her lips.

That way lay madness.

She had to say something. Had to let him know that she was here for business and business only.

She cleared her throat. "I don't care about our past, Ty. Only the future—the one where you act like a respectable celebrity and I get a paycheck for a job well done. The only reason I'm here is to turn you into a decent human being and make sure that photos like these never happen again."

She'd never told so many lies in one breath before.

CHAPTER SIX

Bringing Julie downstairs and surprising her with his art and books had been a stroke of genius.

He was going to have to thank Bobby for the brilliant idea of hiring an image consultant. All these years, part of him had been hoping Julie would materialize in the crowds at a football stadium. Who would have thought Bobby Wilson would be the mastermind behind their long-overdue reunion?

She was so sexy when she got flustered and tried to pretend she wasn't wanting him just as much as he was craving her. Ty couldn't remember the last time he'd had this much fun.

"Okay," he said, his lips an inch from hers. She clearly thought he was about to kiss her, but he couldn't. Not yet, anyway. It was imperative that she kiss him first. Otherwise she'd cry foul, blame him for taking advantage of the situation. "You tell me what I need to do and I'll do it."

Her eyes went wide at his sudden about-face and she looked more than a little disappointed. She'd thought he was about to swoop in and take her lips, taste her, pin her beneath him while she moaned in ecstasy.

A little patience, that's what she needed to learn. Because sometimes drawing out the anticipation was worth the resulting fireworks.

Julie quickly recovered her composure. "Fine. Good. I'm glad we're on the same page. First off, you need some practice looking conservative in pictures."

He raised an eyebrow. "How do you plan to do that?"

"We'll hire a media consultant to train you how to answer questions and pose for photos."

"That's a nice offer, but I don't think a media consultant can help me with my problem."

Her eyebrow arched up. "Which problem would that be? The fact that you're too rich? Or too good-looking? Or, maybe, that you're too successful? Woe is you."

"If you hadn't noticed, women can't resist me."

Her eyes narrowed. "Uh-huh."

"So if they're going to throw themselves at me no matter what I do, you'd better teach me another way to deal with them."

"You mean other than Frenching them in public?"

That little quip was downright snarky—which meant they were finally getting somewhere. He liked to see that bit of fire in her eyes, knowing it would translate into great things in the sack.

And his bed was definitely where they were heading, whether she realized it or not.

"See, that's why your company is so successful. You know exactly how to frame a situation with a few simple words."

"Your point being?"

It shouldn't be this easy. It really shouldn't. "Kisses like this"—he held up the magazine—"are how I've been kissing all my life. It's all I know."

She raised her eyes to the ceiling. "If you were anyone else, I'd know you were joking." He found himself holding his breath for a long second as she paused. "But you, I think, just might be serious."

He held back a smile. An easy five yards on the first down. The next five should be just as easy.

"So, say I'm sitting on a couch with a woman who wants a piece of me. Assume there are cameras and that someone is going to take a picture that ends up in the papers the next day."

"Do you actually think I'm going to do this kind of role-playing with you? I'm starting to wonder what goes on in your alternate reality."

He couldn't help grinning this time. It had been far too long since he'd had such an enjoy-

able conversation with anyone, let alone the oppo-
site sex. His guy friends mostly drank and screwed
around and played video games. And the women
were either trying to get into his pants or his bank
account, or trying to convince him to hook them up
with another football player's bank account and/or
pants.

"Sure," he said. "You've got to be the hot babe.
And then you've got to teach me how to resist you."
He dropped his gaze to her breasts. "Don't worry
that you're all natural. That won't throw me off at all.
Real, fake, as long as they fit right here."

Hoping he could make her laugh instead of walk
out on him, he cupped his hands in the air and moved
them slightly, as if he were holding a soft weight.

"You didn't actually just pretend to squeeze a pair
of breasts, did you?" Fortunately, she looked more
amused than annoyed.

"You know how us jocks are. Now, back to your
role as hot babe."

"As if I'm stupid enough to fall for this."

He was all innocence. "For what?"

She opened her mouth. Then closed it.

Her lower lip was plump and he wanted to
gently sink his teeth into the sensitive flesh, see if
she would shiver, if her nipples would tighten in
response.

The thing was, they both knew he'd painted her

into a corner. Because she sure as hell wasn't going to say, *"You're just trying to get me to kiss you, to sleep with you again."*

Not only was she Little Miss Proper, but she had far too much pride to set herself up for the possibility of being shot down.

She also clearly had no idea that no sane man on earth would shoot her down.

"Fine," she finally said in a tight, pissed-off tone. "The things I do for my company," she muttered. She shook her hair out, stuck out her chest, and pouted at him. "Just as you ordered, one hot babe, hold the side of skank."

Ty had never tried to seduce a woman while he was laughing; fucking had always been more of a serious endeavor. Never a challenge, though—he was always trying to answer the question, "How fast can I leave when we're done?" He very rarely had sex with anyone at his own house. Because it was harder to kick a woman out than it was to zip up his pants and drive away.

"Okay," he said, "throw yourself at me."

"You might find this hard to believe, given that we're in 'Ty's Weird World' right now, but I wouldn't have the first clue how to throw myself at anyone."

"Not even your favorite football star?"

"I don't have a favorite football star," she said. "Or baseball, basketball, or hockey. Gerard Butler is kind of cute, though. Maybe I could pretend you're him?"

Ty wanted to crack Gerard Butler's head against a brick wall. He couldn't believe he was actually jealous of an actor.

Clearly, when it came to Julie Spencer, there was a first time for everything.

"Pretend I'm Gerard Butler, then," he forced out between his teeth.

She held out her hand. "Hi, I'm Julie Spencer. Your movies are really great. Especially that foreign one where you pretend to be the little boy's father."

"That's *it*? What about trying to get in his pants? Where was the flattery? The finger running down his arm? The I-want-to-fuck-you-all-night-long look?"

"You didn't say anything about trying to get in his pants!"

"Duh." He rolled his eyes. "What do you think all of those women in all of those pictures are trying to do to me?"

"It looks like you're trying to get into *their* pants, not the other way around"

He shrugged. "Sometimes I am. But not as often as you'd think."

Which was true. He tended to be a moving target and women just threw and threw and threw themselves at him until one of them stuck for a night.

Ty had never really wanted any one woman in

particular—except for this one. Only Julie. He'd wanted her when he was eighteen, and he wanted her now.

"Try again," he said in his most encouraging voice.

"I still don't see how this is going to help," she argued.

"I'm like an old dog. You've got to teach me new tricks, right?"

She chewed on that for a while. He liked watching her face while her mind worked. It was like she momentarily forgot to be in control of absolutely everything, and when her white teeth came out to bite her lower lip she was sexier than any skimpily dressed model had ever been.

"You're definitely a dog."

He was just going to let that one go. "So it's time to throw yourself at me. Don't worry, I won't laugh."

She glared at him. "The only reason you're not doing this little exercise with one of my assistants is because I can't trust you to behave with any of them."

"Their loss," he said. "I'm waiting. And remember, you're trying to get my pants off."

Sighing in resignation, she fluttered her eyelids and said in a high-pitched baby voice, "Oh Ty, you're just my favorite football player of all time, even though I just slept with a bunch of your teammates last night."

He couldn't help laughing.

More eyelid batting. "I hope this doesn't come across as too forward or anything, but would you mind if I just gave you a teensy-weensy little kiss and let my friend take a picture of it so that everyone will believe me when I say that I kissed the great Ty Calhoun?"

Julie's parody was hitting a little too close to home. How many women had he slept with who actually did talk like this, who had the brain power of an ant?

A little more seriously than he meant to, he said, "Why not? I'm game."

Julie came out of character. "You said you wouldn't laugh at me."

He held his hands up. "Did I laugh?"

"No, but if I'm going to act like an idiot, you can't sit there playing the straight man. You need to play yourself."

"Now you're going to tell me how to play myself? All right, I already know there's no point in trying to stop you. Who am I?"

She waved her hand in the air. "You're the obviously jaded yet horny sports star. You only think about your own needs, but you're more than willing to bump and grind with a pretty stranger after a good game to celebrate."

Ty couldn't think of the last time anyone had said anything that unflattering to his face.

"You really believe that's how I am, don't you?"

She frowned, possibly noticing for the first time that she was hurting his feelings with her blunt assessments.

Or maybe she was doing it on purpose. Revenge and all that.

"It's not just you, Ty. All sports stars are exactly the same."

Ty wanted to disagree, wanted to tell her about all the guys he knew who spent more time taking care of their families, their friends, and the underprivileged than they did their own health. He wanted to tell her that his friend Tim had gotten out on that field every day for ten years as a defensive tackle and let the other team beat his body all to hell, out of sheer desperation to help his whole extended family rise up out of the trash heap of a town they'd been living in.

He knew guys who treated football like any other job. They put in the hours, gave their all, and then they went home for dinner with their wives and children. They didn't waste time in bars or hanging out with groupies. They earned their money with quiet power.

But he knew there wasn't any point in trying to change her mind about professional athletes, or about him. Not when she'd made up her mind long ago.

Plus, he had to admit that she wasn't too far off

the mark for many of the guys he knew. Even, at the start of his career, himself.

He ran his fingers through his hair. "Okay then, I'll play the highly stereotyped version of myself."

He gave her a hard, hungry look.

"A kiss from you is what I've been waiting for my entire life, baby. Come sit on my lap—but only if you're not wearing anything under that short skirt."

She pushed her thighs together, a nearly imperceptible movement that he might have missed if he weren't so attuned to her. Or, more precisely, how much he wanted her.

"That's better," she said. "We'll skip the kiss and get straight to working on your reaction."

He wasn't going to let her get away with that. "Not realistic enough. I thought role-playing only worked if everyone gave themselves over to their characters?"

Her expression said it all. He was right. She was going to have to kiss him in order to teach him the "right" way to behave around overzealous fans.

"Fine," she snapped, and then a few sweet moments later she had transformed again into Wonder-Babe. She slid next to him, thigh to thigh. Was it pathetic that he actually started sweating? Just because he could feel her leg through his jeans?

Yes. It was.

She threaded her hands through his hair and pulled his head down to hers. But at the last second, she looked up into his eyes. In an instant, Wonder-Babe disappeared, leaving Julie behind.

It was that last-second pause that almost did him in. He wanted her. Now. He wanted to take her mouth, could practically taste her.

Tentatively, she pressed her lips to his. A million bolts of lightning shot through him.

It nearly killed him to hold still. *Please,* he begged, hardly able to believe that he was actually praying, *please don't let her stop.*

Ty had never been completely certain if any of his prayers on the field had really been answered before, or if he'd just pulled a clutch play out of his ass at the last moment by blind luck. But when Julie began to explore the contours of his mouth with her own, as her tongue came out to taste the corner where his upper and lower lip met, he became a believer in the power of prayer.

Her breath was soft and sweet and he didn't want to move a muscle, didn't want to do anything that would mess up this perfect moment. Her mouth moved to his cheek, to the beginnings of his stubble. One of her hands moved from his hair to his cheek to his neck; then she rubbed her thumb over the hollow beneath his collarbone, then found that skin with her lips.

A groan nearly escaped his lungs, but somehow he held it in. Again she found his mouth, and this time she was less tentative. Her tongue came out, teased him again, sliding into him.

He couldn't keep from devouring her for another second. Just as he was on the verge of taking control of the situation, she stopped kissing him, stopped exploring him with her mouth and hands.

She wouldn't meet his eyes.

"On the contrary, Ty, I don't think I need to teach you anything at all." She sounded like she was going to choke. "You did very well."

If he could have gotten words out of his own constricted lungs, he would have. At long last, he managed a strangled, "Are you kidding me?"

Her eyes met his. "You were the perfect gentleman. Good job."

"Do you have any idea how much I want you right now?" he growled. "And not because of some stupid role-playing. Or because I wish you were a groupie."

She shook her head, tried to pick up her briefcase, then watched in horror as it slipped from her fingers and slid beneath his coffee table.

"I can't do this," she whispered and he wasn't sure if he was listening in on her private thoughts or if she'd meant to speak aloud.

All Ty could think as he stared at her was, *I have wanted you every single day, every minute, every second since the last time I saw you.*

Was that true? Did he really think that?

Oh shit. He did. Now that she was sitting here, right in front of him, now that she'd kissed him, he knew the truth.

If she knew how he really felt she'd hold her power over him like a shiny butcher knife and plunge it into his heart to exact the retribution she felt she deserved.

"Don't go," he said instead of admitting the stupid, swirling truth.

CHAPTER SEVEN

She couldn't leave. No matter how desperately she needed to, Ty was her first kiss. Her first orgasm. Her first morning in bed with someone else.

The one night she'd spent with Ty had guided her sensuality for more than a decade. She'd tried to avoid men like him, but lost the battle. She'd dated unassuming men, but always ended up having sexual affairs with charismatic charmers.

Yet no one, regardless of how successful or funny or charming they were, had ever come close to matching the few hours she'd spent in Ty's arms.

Only a fool would have actually kissed him in the name of "role-playing."

How could she have forgotten that shame and desire made such a horrible pair? And that desire always won?

She hadn't been able to stop herself. And so she'd licked him and bit at him and he'd done nothing.

Nothing.

Then he'd said, *"Do you have any idea how much I want you right now?"* and foolish hope had leaped to life within her.

She was an adult this time. She could take what she wanted from him and walk away in one piece, couldn't she?

Maybe a kiss was just the thing to break the sensual flight pattern they were in. In all likelihood, they'd both look at each other and realize they'd been building the whole grad night thing into a much bigger deal than it really was.

Once they got the kiss out of the way, they'd simply work together to rebuild Ty's image into one his boss approved of and then they'd happily go their separate ways.

Yeah right, said her heart, but she wasn't listening. She was too busy hoping she could convince him to make good on all that "wanting her" business.

She boldly threw press photos at him, one after another. "I can't believe I have to remind you how you *really* kiss your fans. How can I teach you how to behave if you don't act like you normally do?"

The corner of his mouth moved and something akin to relief ran through his eyes.

"I've always respected a woman who takes her work seriously."

"Thank you," she said and then the next moment he'd pulled her onto his lap and was stealing her breath from her lungs.

His tongue invaded her mouth and taught hers how to dance again while his big, strong hands cupped her bottom.

"Is that better?" he murmured as he dragged his mouth down to the ultra-sensitive spot at the base of her ear.

She couldn't answer; he was setting her entire body on fire. Thankfully, his hands were just as naughty as his mouth. She felt the heat of his palm through her tailored shirt a millisecond before his thumb brushed across her nipple.

Her body sprang to desperate attention beneath his skilled touch. She reached for him, cupped his heart-stoppingly beautiful face in her hands, and kissed him. All the while that he was fondling her and stroking her and sliding down zippers and undoing buttons, she was losing herself in his kiss.

She couldn't think clearly when he was kissing her, when he was replacing her removed shirt with his mouth, kissing her collarbone, heading for the spot between her breasts as he unhooked her bra.

Finally—oh God, it couldn't be soon enough—he was cupping her breasts in both hands, squeezing them together, laving her nipples with his tongue, with the rough bristles of his jaw, his cheeks.

Funny little gasps were coming from her throat, but she couldn't stop them, any more than she could stop herself from growing wet and heavy between her legs. She was this close to begging him to slip one hand beneath her skirt, her panties. One touch and she'd explode. That was all she wanted.

Ty was all she wanted.

His voice drifted up from between her breasts, low and ragged. "You have the most beautiful body I've ever seen."

Julie arched her breasts against him, shifted so that her skirt bunched up at her waist, and straddled him.

She settled down onto his heavy, jean-clad erection with a moan of satisfaction. All she wanted to do was press herself into him like this while he sucked at her breasts.

With a groan, he pulled her even closer against him. Julie loved everything: the way he was whispering her name again and again as he licked and nipped the sensitive skin on her breasts; the way his jeans felt rough against the mostly exposed skin beneath her fishnet stockings; the way she'd never felt so wet, so aroused, so full of need that she was almost bursting from it.

She was close, so close to the satisfaction she'd been

missing all these years. She could see the peak, was climbing straight toward it, when Ty said, "Oh no, you don't," and flipped her onto her back on the couch.

She blinked up at him, disoriented and bewildered. Hadn't she just been about to come, with Ty beneath her? Quickly, he answered her silent question.

"My jeans are not getting the pleasure that I want for myself," he said as he stripped her skirt off.

Her shoes were already gone and slowly, with a patience she wished he didn't have, he slid her stockings over her hips, past her aching clit, down her incredibly sensitive thighs, and finally over her knees and calves and the soles of her feet.

A part of her wanted to yell, "Hurry," but before she could give in to the urge, Ty said, "I like your panties."

Lingerie was her biggest splurge. Silk from France, lace from Italy. She hadn't bought it to turn on the men she slept with; she simply liked the feel of luxurious, sensual fabrics against her skin. It was her way of acknowledging the sexy woman within her.

"I like you better naked, though," he said as he slid her panties off and dropped them onto the plush rug.

All she wanted was for him to slip his finger inside her—that's all it would take. But he'd never followed the rules. Not in school, not on the field, and not now.

His mouth came down hot and heavy on her pussy lips and her hips bucked up to meet him. Strong, calloused hands cupped her ass, pulled her closer. Julie's body instantly obeyed his command, and she pushed into his teeth, his tongue.

And then his fingers found her, slipped and slid against her clit, against her engorged lips, and then finally, deep within.

"Ty," she moaned, his name a prayer of wonder as the first waves knocked her down. No orgasm had ever been this intense, not even back in high school on the yacht.

She tried to prepare herself for the next hit of plea-sure, but she couldn't, she didn't have the resources against the constant onslaught of Ty's tongue, fin-gers, the way he pushed into her clit, then backed away, only to give her more and send her higher.

Her brain ceased to function as he rode her harder and harder with his hands, higher and higher with his mouth.

Then, miraculously, her brain pushed through the fog of sensation. Where had this girl come from, the one who would do anything for that orgasm? All these years, she'd been in hiding. Ever since the night when this bad boy broke her heart.

In an instant, the spell of lust collapsed.

With superhuman strength, she pushed him onto the far end of the couch. As she scrambled into her clothes—even though she knew his eyes never left her face, not for one second, even though she knew how hard he was behind the zipper of his jeans, even though they were both panting from what had just happened—she wouldn't let herself look at his face. Into his eyes.

If she so much as glanced up into his beautiful eyes and all the desire in them, she'd leap onto his lap and ride him like she was going for a gold medal.

"I can't do this anymore." She ran up the stairs, her shoes and briefcase in her hands. "You'll have to work with Amy. She'll call you with the new plan."

She tried to turn the knob to get the hell away from him, but it was locked. With wild determination, she pounded at the keypad with her fists.

"Open, goddamnit!" she yelled.

Ty moved behind her to punch in the code, and when the door beeped open, she leaped through it and out to her car with a speed she hadn't known she possessed.

She could never, ever see Ty again.

Never.

CHAPTER EIGHT

Ty was painfully hard.

He wasn't surprised that Julie had fled before they could finish the deed. And really, he decided as he turned the shower on cold, he'd thoroughly enjoyed himself anyway. Because even though he hadn't had the pleasure of sliding into her hot, slick pussy, he'd gotten his rocks off in other ways.

Just kissing her was lethal.

And those breasts. A guy could lose himself in how soft her skin was, in the way her nipples tasted.

And then there was the fact that she had the most beautiful pussy in all creation.

The icy water temporarily worked its magic on his libido, so he wrapped a towel around his waist and thought about his next move.

She didn't want to work with him anymore, but he

wanted to be with her. What was the one thing absolutely guaranteed to bring Julie running to his side? And, if all went really well, keep her there?

He grinned with sudden certainty. He knew exactly what he needed to do. Oh yes, he'd be seeing Julie again very soon.

＊

Julie walked into Amy's office, closed the blinds, and threw herself down on the overstuffed chair in the corner.

Amy stopped typing. "Uh-oh. What's wrong?"

"I just did a very bad thing."

"How bad?"

Julie bit her lip. She was the boss. She was supposed to set an example of professional behavior. And what had she done?

"I slept with a client."

Amy was out of her seat and sitting on the coffee table in front of Julie within seconds. "You didn't."

Julie nodded, miserable and yet still energized and tingly from the amazing orgasm Ty had bestowed upon her just minutes ago.

"Oh yes, I most certainly did."

Amy's face was a picture of disbelief. "Who could you have possibly slept with? Honestly, I can't think of a single one of our clients without their clothes on." She paused. "Thank God."

Her voice barely above a whisper, Julie admitted, "We got a new client this morning. Remember?"

"This morning? The only people who called today were from that football team. The Outlaws."

Amy's eyes grew big with sudden comprehension. Julie didn't say anything, just waited for her friend to do some quick math over which Outlaw player was most likely to need an image consultant.

"Ty Calhoun?" Amy's voice notched up a note. "No freakin' way. You couldn't have. You hate football. You hate sports stars. Even incredibly hot ones like him." She fanned herself. "Damn, that man is hot."

Amy didn't know about Julie's past with Ty; no one did. She'd never wanted to admit even to her closest friend that she'd been so naïve, so pathetically in love with someone who would never ever love her back. The time had come for confessing.

"Promise you won't hate me for not telling you about this before. I'm not good at telling secrets. Especially ones that make me look stupid." She paused for a long moment. "The thing is, I used to know Ty Calhoun. A long time ago."

"When? I've known you since college, met practically every guy you ever dated. And I definitely would have remembered if he'd taken you out."

"We went to high school together."

"Oh."

Julie was amazed how many meanings one short word could have.

"We didn't hang out. Not until the graduation party."

Amy put her hand over her heart in empathy. "Please tell me he wasn't the guy you chose to lose your virginity to."

Julie had never felt more stupid. "Everything seemed so different that night. He was different. Needless to say, things didn't work out between us."

"So that explains why we never take the athletic contracts." Amy went into problem-solving mode. "What do you need me to do for you?"

Julie had never appreciated her best friend and right-hand woman more. "I can't see him again."

"I guessed. And I'm also guessing that you don't want to hook the Outlaws up with a new company, right?"

"Of course not. I need the money, for the building."

"Okay then, consider Ty my problem from now on." Amy grinned. "And you can be absolutely certain that I will exact painful revenge upon him for hurting you."

Finally, Julie found a smile. "Good. And thank you."

Amy fiddled with her wedding ring for a few seconds, and Julie knew what she wanted to ask.

"Since I know you're wondering," she told her friend, "it was great."

Amy laughed, helping Julie finally break out of her self-pity. "Thank you for telling me. I've been married for so long, I need to live vicariously through you."

The rest of the day, as Julie threw herself into her work, she waited for relief to wash over her. Ty was Amy's problem now. They'd conduct all of their meetings outside the office; Amy would accompany him to charity events; she'd be the one teaching him how to give his fans a chaste peck on the cheek in front of the cameras, or better yet, a handshake.

But relief never came. Instead, during her South Beach Diet meal for one that evening, she found herself worrying about Ty's effect on her best friend. Could any woman really withstand that charm, the sensual power he wielded? What if Amy fell for him? Ty was the ultimate woman magnet—even an intelligent, married woman like Amy wouldn't be able to help herself. What if Ty came between Amy and her husband, Jon? Julie would never forgive herself for pawning him off on her friend if that happened. If she'd had a male employee, she would have passed Ty off to him in an instant.

Julie hated how inadequate everything about her life and her business seemed a mere twelve hours after Ty had swaggered back into her life. She'd been happy, damn it. She'd enjoyed quiet nights at home, pleasant dates, occasional affairs that quickly fizzled out. How boring it now seemed in comparison to him. His house was an all-day party, and even his private underground room outdid her sleek, unfussy home across from Golden Gate Park.

Unable to sleep that night, she didn't know why she'd even bothered going to bed. She tried to convince herself that her excess energy was nothing more than anger at the way Ty had manipulated her into being with him again, but every cell in her body called her a liar.

She had taken the job, gone to his house, let him take her clothes off all because she wanted to be with him again. She'd been so desperate for more sex with him that she'd been perfectly willing to give up all of the principles by which she lived her life. Just like the first time.

How was it that five seconds with Ty made her lose hold of everything she was? Everything she'd worked so hard to build?

And worse, why did she want nothing more than to have him here with her, in her bed, making her call out his name? Especially when she'd vowed never to be in the same room with him ever again?

✳

Ty was bored. Strip clubs had been a lot of fun when he was twenty-one, but as the years went by, he felt more and more like a dirty old man watching young dancers shimmy in their G-strings and tassels. He'd had more than his fair share of groupies, stuffed twenties into countless G-strings. The women's faces all started to blur together after a while.

Still, he tried to look like he was having a good time. After all, that was the whole point of tonight. He'd called his friends and told them to meet him at the Hustler Club. It was imperative that he be surrounded by a party and plenty of naked women, that people got drunk enough to whip out their cell phones and take pictures of him.

Somebody would try to make some money off the shot, and then he'd have Julie right where he wanted her.

Until then, he supposed he'd have to keep stuffing dollar bills into the dancers' G-strings, maybe even get a lap dance or two, make some personal sacrifices just to keep up the ruse.

He grinned, already looking forward to seeing her bright and early tomorrow morning in Bobby's office.

The phone rang at 7:00 A.M., waking Julie out of a deep sleep. Saturday was the only day she allowed herself to sleep later than sunrise. But since she hadn't actually fallen asleep until what felt like a few minutes ago, she was completely disoriented when she picked up the phone.

A southern drawl was the last thing she expected. "Ms. Spencer?"

She quickly sat up in bed, pushed her hair back from her face. No way could the new owner of the Outlaws calling her bright and early on a Saturday morning be a good thing. She swallowed past the sawdust in her mouth.

"Speaking."

"I believe I hired you to reform the finest player on my team?"

What had Ty done? Because whatever it was, she had to hand it to him: He'd gotten the big guns to come out shooting.

Right at her chest.

"Yes, sir," she said. "Mr. Calhoun and I met briefly yesterday to go over our preliminary plan."

"Did your plan include late-night visits to strip clubs, my dear?"

Strip clubs? Oh, God! Shock and hurt hit her square across the chest. He'd gone from her nearly naked body straight to a stranger's naked body.

She knew she didn't mean anything to him, but it hurt to have it slap her in the face.

Before she managed to get her brain around a reply, he said, "We're in my office waiting for you. Aren't we, Mr. Calhoun?"

From a distance, she heard Ty call out, "Hey, Julie. You missed a real fun time last night."

His nerve was almost as enormous as his ego.

"I'm on my way," she bit out, but the phone was already dead in her hands.

While she set a speed record for showering, getting dressed, and putting on makeup, Julie imagined all the different ways she could murder Ty. But nothing she could think of was either gory enough or involved enough prolonged torture to suit her.

She wanted blood and by God, she was going to get it.

CHAPTER NINE

Good morning, sunshine."

The smile that Julie pinned on her face nearly disintegrated in the face of Ty's cheerful, too-gorgeous-for-his-own-good-and-hers-too greeting.

After a night of carousing, it just wasn't fair that he should look so good. He was still an irresistible bundle of muscles and heat, his long tanned fingers stroking the arm of his chair, as if he wished he was caressing skin rather than cold leather.

At least she presented a pretty picture in front of her nemesis and the very powerful, rather unattractive man who'd hired her to perform a miracle. She'd known plenty of men like Bobby Wilson—men who prided themselves on wielding power in the most distressing way possible. Without fail, the women who bested these men were not simply beautiful to a fault, they were feminine and ever-gracious as well.

Her blouse was appealing without being overtly sexy, and if ever there was a time for the little pink skirt that swished around her knees and the shoes with the cute bows on the back of the heel, this meeting was it.

"I sure hope I didn't disturb your beauty sleep, Ms. Spencer," Bobby said.

Julie didn't believe him for one second. He would love to know that he'd wrecked her entire life with his phone call.

"It was a pleasure to hear from you," she said, letting her hand be enveloped by his damp one.

Bobby's handshake was limp, like a dead fish. Lovely.

She turned her smile up brighter, confident in her ability to charm the team's owner. Ty wasn't the only one with charisma in his corner. The difference was, she carefully chose who to dole it out to.

"Please, have a seat," Bobby said, gesturing to an upholstered seat that was far too close to Ty for Julie's liking. But then, the same state was too close for comfort where he was concerned.

She sat down and crossed her legs, far more pleased at the blatant appreciation in Ty's eyes than she should have been. Although she'd dressed to impress Bobby, she wasn't averse to Ty drooling over her—and all the things he was *never* going to get to touch and kiss again—as well.

Bobby looked between Julie and Ty. "Well, if the

two of you aren't the prettiest pair outside of a Miss America contest."

Julie was disconcerted. Was there any way to graciously deflect that?

Ty said, "Come on now, boss, we both know I don't hold a candle to Julie."

Damn it, he wasn't supposed to compliment her, defending her from his horrible boss as well.

Bobby sat on the edge of his antique desk, which creaked beneath him. "Too bad I couldn't have met you under nicer circumstances, Ms. Spencer."

Her heart thumped in alarm, but Julie was a pro at presenting an outwardly calm demeanor. With quiet patience, she waited for Bobby to continue.

"You see, pretty lady, I believed that hiring you as this young stud's image consultant meant that my days of dealing with his embarrassing public displays of affection for well-endowed young ladies had come to an end."

She nodded. "Of course you did."

"I'm nothing if not a fair man," he said. "That's why I'm happy to give you a chance to explain what caused these pictures to be taken last night."

He handed her a stack of pages printed from various internet gossip sites. In each and every one of them, Ty was cavorting with women with impossibly large breasts and small waists.

Ty leaned over the arm of his seat to look at the

pictures. "My hair is getting kind of long, don't you think? Might need to get a trim soon."

Was he fucking *kidding* her? She'd nearly let him have sex with her yesterday at his house, and now that she was looking at pictures of him with other naked women, did he truly expect her to calmly sit there and comment on his hair?

Fine. Two could play that game. "I'm sure these women could give you tips on how to deal with unwanted hair."

He sat back looking extremely smug. "I've always appreciated a good Brazilian."

Julie's face flamed before she could stop it. There was no point in making excuses to her new boss; it was always better to tell the truth in impossible-client situations like this. "I'm afraid, Mr. Wilson, that Mr. Calhoun is a bit of a wild card."

Bobby nodded, clearly pleased by her pronouncement. "Why don't you just say what we're all thinking? He's a disaster."

Ty interrupted. "We're not all thinking that."

Julie smiled sweetly and looked at Ty. "Oh yes, we are."

"Now, darlin'," Bobby continued, "if you don't have the skills to keep this wild child of mine under control, then you might as well resign right now."

Never. Julie had always completed each and every assignment beautifully. No problem was too big, no personality too outlandish for her to shine up and present to the public as a new man or woman. But she knew simply stating her case wouldn't matter to a cretin like Bobby. She'd have to utilize her "pretty" card.

She slowly re-crossed her legs, letting her skirt hike up a slight bit, then moved her ankle up, then down, doing her Christian Louboutin heels proud.

She let her voice go a little breathless. "Now, Mr. Wilson, we both know I have no intention of resigning from this account."

Unsurprisingly, Bobby's eyes didn't make it much farther than her thighs.

She continued, "From this moment forward, you can count on me to be personally responsible for Ty's reputation. I will guard it as if it were my own."

Bobby continued his lazy perusal of her assets one last time. "Ms. Spencer, I must say, you certainly paint a persuasive picture."

She smiled. Though such shallow tactics disgusted her, she was too smart not to use them when necessary.

"There's only one problem that I can see." Bobby bared his teeth at her in an approximation of a smile. "I just don't see how any one person—especially a woman, no offense meant, darlin'—is going to be able to control our wild boy. Not without an airtight plan."

Her professional reputation was at stake here,

along with paying her new mortgage for the next several months.

A sudden calm washed over her, and she clasped her hands together on her lap.

"Ty will be moving in with me this morning. For the next two weeks I won't let him out of my sight. Not for a workout, a meal, a charitable event. Nothing."

She couldn't worry about Ty's reaction now, she'd deal with him later. Possibly with a sharp stick.

Bobby looked skeptical. "You on board with this, Superstar?" he asked Ty.

Slouched in his chair, Ty reached his arms back behind his head, stretched, then yawned.

"I didn't get much sleep last night," he finally said. "I'm looking forward to a big breakfast, and a soft bed." He raised an eyebrow in Julie's direction. "I figure your bed is as good as mine."

In that moment, Julie was thankful for everything she had ever learned from her parents about faking it. Otherwise, she would have launched herself across the room and strangled Ty.

"I have a lovely guest room all set up for you," she lied, then reached out to shake Bobby's hand. "I'm glad this is all settled. It was a pleasure to meet you."

How the hell was she going to keep her legs shut around Ty 24-7 for two whole weeks?

CHAPTER TEN

Ty left Bobby's office a very happy man. And not just because Julie's skirt served her ass up on a platter. If he'd known that a pack of strippers could get him into Julie's bed—who was she kidding with that guest bedroom crap?—this fast, he would have sent her a stripper-gram years ago.

Still, he wasn't a complete asshole, no matter what she thought. "They were just pictures," he said when they stepped outside.

She didn't even bother turning around to face him, just kept walking through the Outlaws' parking lot. "I really don't care."

Which meant she did, of course. It was too bad he had to act like an oversexed jerk to make sure they were together for the next two weeks, but that was the only way for them to get to know each other better. The only chance they had at a relationship.

He stopped, blinking in the bright sunlight off the Bay. What the hell was he doing, thinking in terms of a relationship? He'd never thought any further than one night. What was it about Julie that had him thinking crazy and acting even crazier?

"Get in," she said, pointing to a Prius sedan.

He strolled around the tiny hybrid car.

"I doubt I'm going to fit," he said suggestively.

Her face set into a grim mask. Shit. Too late, he remembered that she'd said nearly those exact words about him ten years ago, right before he took her virginity.

Okay, time for apologies. And he'd start by leaving his Maserati in the parking lot and squeezing into her itsy-bitsy environmentally correct car.

"Julie, I didn't just mean what you thought I meant," he said as she drove out toward Bay Street.

She glared at him. "I'm going to say this one more time, so try to get it through your thick skull. I don't care what you meant. Or what you thought you meant. Or what you did last night with a stack of over-endowed strippers. Or how you did everything in your power to humiliate me in front of Bobby. I just don't *care*, Ty."

In the blink of an eye, she pulled herself back together. "I. Don't. Care." To the naked eye she seemed composed and calm.

But he was more attuned to her than that, and he could feel her simmering beneath the surface.

"The only thing I care about," she continued, "is you making a good impression. My only concern is to transform the way the public sees you. Bye-bye, wild child."

Because he owed her one, he chose not to say something that would annoy her again. Yet. "You handled Bobby well."

It wasn't an empty compliment; he really did think she'd played his smarmy boss well. Playing up her looks had been a brillant tactic.

"Jocks," she sniffed. "I swear to God, if you want them to remember something you need to write it on the back of their hand. So here it is again; I am not interested in your opinion."

Too bad. She was getting the compliment whether she wanted it or not.

"Guys like Bobby aren't easy men to negotiate with. But you had him wrapped around your little finger." He looked down at her legs, her sexy shoes. God, she was hot.

"Sure I did. That's why I ended up having to live with you for the next two weeks." Sarcasm dripped from every word.

"You're living the dream," he said, only partly mocking himself.

"Don't kid yourself," she said, laughing. "The women you hang out with want to spend your money and be seen with you and be serviced by you in bed. Living with you is a price they have to pay."

He grinned, even though she probably was right. "If the rewards are big enough . . ." he said. By the way she dropped the conversation, he figured he'd won.

They pulled into his driveway. "Pack your bags and be quick about it. On second thought," she said, studying his clothes like he was a bug smashed flat under a microscope, "I don't think you can be trusted with this task. I'll pack your bags."

What the hell? She had to be the only person on earth who had a problem with the way he dressed. Ty knew he looked great in his Cavalli shirt and Diesel jeans.

She walked in his open front door and asked one of his buddies, who'd just come from the hot tub, "Which way to his bedroom?" She jerked a thumb in Ty's direction.

Jack looked at Ty, then looked at Julie, and quickly figured out who the boss was. "Last door down the hall to the left."

"Thanks." Julie headed through his house as if she owned it.

"Dude, you have all the luck," his friend said.

"Don't I know it," Ty said, grinning. And he was going to get even luckier.

"You should really charge a fee," she said when he caught up to her in the hallway, then stopped at the threshold of his bedroom so suddenly, he nearly plowed into her.

The decorating was a little over the top, but what did he care? The master suite was for shut-eye and sex. Besides, the women he brought back seemed to expect every stop to be pulled out: 800-thread-count sheets, a roaring fireplace, views, a deck, a bathtub big enough for half his team, a shower with ten jets.

The best part of all was that he'd bought the house with cash.

Which meant no one could take it away from him.

Julie was holding on to the door frame so tightly, her knuckles had gone white. Somehow he had a feeling she wasn't bowled over by the opulence. She'd grown up in a fancy house.

She must be freaking out over the bed, probably having dirty thoughts about what she wanted to do to him between the sheets.

If he wanted to move into her good graces, and thus her bed, he needed to stop messing with her. But he'd been acting like a smart-ass for way too long to stop himself now.

Putting his hand on the small of her back, he gently pushed her into the room. He walked over to the bed, which his housekeeper hadn't made yet. Tucking a pillow back up against the antique wrought-iron headboard, he looked up at her.

"I could use a little help here."

She blinked, her eyes faintly wild. "With what?"

"The bed."

She took a step back and he gave her a knowing look.

"Has anyone ever told you that you have a dirty mind?"

In an instant she became the prim Little Miss Perfect he remembered from high school. "Of course not," she snapped.

"All I'm asking you to do is help me make the bed."

He watched her war with herself and realize that she couldn't refuse his request. It would only make her seem like she really did have a dirty mind.

She walked over to the other side of the bed and shoved his sheets into place with ill grace. She threw the duvet cover onto her half of the bed, then spun around and made a beeline for his walk-in closet.

"No, no, no, and most definitely no," she said as she shoved hangers around, taking her anger out on his clothes. "Do you even *own* anything appropriate?"

"If you mean boring, then no."

She waved dismissively at all of his clothes. "You can't wear any of this. Not if we ever expect you to be taken seriously."

He was surprised that she was turning her nose up at his designer clothes; she knew quality when she saw it. So what was her problem?

"Don't worry about what Bobby said," he teased. "You'll still look better than me, no matter what I'm wearing."

She looked up toward the ceiling as if praying for guidance. "It's my job to make sure that you don't look like you should have a pop starlet hanging off your arm who's been buying your clothes off a runway."

Not the most flattering picture, but it drove the point home.

"Have you been to a funeral recently?" she asked.

One corner of his mouth curved up. "Is that a hint?"

She furrowed her brow before realization dawned in her blue eyes. "Maybe," she said, "but only if you give me any trouble."

He liked it when she teased him back. He crooked a finger at her to follow him.

"This way."

He took her into a small closet in a room across the hall, one where they both barely fit. He liked the vibe in here, the two of them so very close. She smelled flowery, yet sultry. He wanted to pull her close, breathe in her hair, push it to the side, taste her neck, find out all over again where her most sensitive spots were. He wanted to push back one of those boring suits she was going to go nuts over and take her hard and fast against the wall. He could already picture her legs wrapped around his waist, her head thrown back, how damn good it would feel when he slid into her.

"Thank God," she said as she pulled out a basic navy pinstriped suit. "I was worried you didn't have any clothes that didn't scream pimp."

That snapped him out of his extremely pleasant fantasy. Though maybe she did have a point. He'd never been all that comfortable in the designer clothes that his stylist picked out for him. He hadn't even wanted a stylist in the first place, but his agent had insisted.

Clearly, having Julie around wasn't all bad. Especially if she could do some dirty work for him.

"My stylist isn't going to be too happy with you."

She handed him several conservative suits. "She's fired."

He held back a grin. Who else did he need to get rid of? The guy who cut his hair was kind of annoying too.

"Bring these out, then grab anything else you need," she said. "I'll be waiting in your living room."

He hadn't realized until now how sick he was of everyone doing his bidding without question. It also kind of got his motor running to be bossed around by her. Still, keeping her on her toes was an important part of the dance she probably didn't even realize they were doing.

"I've got some bathing suits that you might fit into if you want to hang out by the pool."

The disgusted look on her face was so cute, he nearly grabbed her and kissed it off.

"First of all, I wouldn't wear one of the thong bikinis from one of your 'girlfriends' "—she put the word in quotes—"if everything else I owned went up in flames."

He nodded. "That's cool. I get it. Girls with dirty minds like you always want to skinny-dip."

She ignored his dig. "You have fifteen minutes to get your stuff together, then we're out of here."

"Just one problem with that," he said.

She sighed a big, chest-heaving sigh that did magnificent things to her breasts. "Why am I not surprised that there's a problem? What is it this time?"

"Bobby's impromptu meeting cut into my workout, and working out is part of my job description."

"How long will that take?"

"A hundred laps usually takes forty-five minutes. I could sprint some of them if you're in a rush to get somewhere."

"No," she said, "We've got all the time in the world."

Wrong. Two weeks wasn't nearly enough time to convince her to give in to what she really wanted.

Him.

In her bed.

∗

Julie couldn't remember the last time she'd felt so off-kilter.

So emotional.

So horny.

He wasn't nearly as dumb as she wished he was. She needed to stop freaking out over every little thing, thereby giving him endless ammo to hold over her.

In the past twenty-four hours she'd been angrier, happier, and more satisfied than she'd been in the past ten years combined.

All because of Ty—damn him.

When she'd seen his massive iron bed, she'd been hit by breathtaking images of them rolling around naked on it. It made a demon inside her leap to life, one who wanted to be tied up by Ty, who got hot at the thought of lying naked on his bed, her arms up over her head bound by a silk tie. She'd practically heard herself begging him to take her, harder, faster.

Enough!

From this moment forward, she was going to keep her hormones in check. Even if he made her scream in ecstasy, he'd leave her heart stone cold in the morning.

Julie sat on a chaise lounge and put her feet up

on the soft cushions. She pulled a pen and a leather-bound notepad out of her bag, deciding to use Ty's workout time to make some notes on her plans for his transformation rather than worrying and drooling over him.

But just as she put pen to paper, Ty emerged from the house. She'd thought his washboard stomach at eighteen was impressive, but the hard, rippling, muscles mere feet from her now were beyond anything she could have imagined.

She lost her breath somewhere between the deep indents of his abdominal muscles and the line of dark hair running from his navel into his low-slung swim shorts. She tried to look away, but she couldn't help but appreciate the beautiful cut of his triceps, the play of the muscles on his back, and the deep valley between his shoulders.

The tip of her pen dug into her palm but she didn't feel it, too busy trying to deal with the lust coursing through her.

She burned to touch him. She yearned to taste him, to run her tongue over the hills and valleys of his incredibly hard abs.

She pulled her gaze up to his eyes, expecting to see victory there. He had to know the kind of power he held over her.

But instead of triumph, something dark and heady simmered in his dark brown eyes. Something that told her he wanted her as much as she wanted him.

A soft voice inside her whispered, *Take what you want. Use him the way he used you.*

She scrambled off the chair, nearly turning her ankle on the flagstone patio. She *couldn't* give in to what her body wanted. She had to remember how bad he was for her.

"Julie," he said, his voice a caress.

She picked up her bag and held it in front of her like a shield. "Go swim. *Please.*"

✳

Ty was an eighty-five-degree pool kind of guy, but today he needed a cold mountain lake to cool off.

Julie wasn't ready—that was the problem. It was one thing to seduce her in his underground refuge yesterday; he'd wanted to prove to her that she wasn't immune to him, no matter what she professed. But maybe, just maybe, this wasn't a game anymore.

What if he really wanted her to stick around? Then what?

He finished his laps and shook off like a dog before reaching for his towel. He'd had a hard-on that wouldn't quit since he'd first walked into her office. Frankly, it was getting old.

Without saying a word to her, he headed into the shower. He couldn't believe he was about to take care of himself when there was a beautiful woman in his house. He hadn't had to do that since he was a teenager.

Hot water blasted over him as he leaned against the tiles, then reached for his cock and pictured her naked in the shower with him, water running over her perfect tits, licking the drops off her nipples. He'd follow the streaming water running over her belly, between her legs with his hand. He'd slip one finger in her, and she'd be tight and wet and he'd drop to his knees and pull her pussy into his mouth, force his tongue into her, hard and fast until she was screaming. Then just as she started to come, he'd pull her down on top of him and she'd take his cock all the way inside, while their bodies slipped wet and hot against each other. Ty roared in the glass and tile confines of his shower as come spilled into his hand.

Next time, it wouldn't be a fantasy. He wouldn't be doing this by himself.

He'd be inside Julie.

CHAPTER ELEVEN

Julie wanted to feel safe again, and the one place she'd always felt totally at ease was at work. Then again, she'd never had a six-foot-two bundle of muscle and sensuality prowling around her office. Even her employees had been reduced to quivering masses of hormones when she'd introduced Ty—and these were smart, savvy women.

She checked email and tried to ignore Ty snooping around her bookshelf, her artwork, her desk.

"You built this business all by yourself?"

She looked up from her keyboard. "Of course I did."

"No need to get all defensive. It was just a question."

She bit back a protest. He was right; she *was* acting defensive. It was just that everyone always assumed her parents had helped her out. But she never took their friends as clients. Her business success depended entirely on how she and her employees performed. Not because she was Daddy's little girl, or because Mommy took her shopping for clients at society teas.

"I love what I do," she finally said.

He nodded. "Me too. It's a good thing to like your job. Beats the hell out of hating it."

An actual conversation that wasn't loaded with double entendres. She wasn't sure she was comfortable with that, actually. At least when they were sniping at each other, everything made sense.

Better keep on your guard, she told herself yet again.

Her front door opened and her receptionist hissed, "Rachel Noah's here," into her intercom.

"Oh shit," she muttered under her breath. Rachel held the strings to some big new political clients. "Please be nice to her," she begged Ty. "Say all the right things. Just this once."

He raised an eyebrow. "One kiss."

She barely had time to process his request, to understand that a barter was being made.

"Okay. One. Now don't screw this up."

Julie smiled and greeted Rachel just outside her office door. "I'm so glad you're here," she said.

Rachel looked like she'd been sucking lemons. "Amy told my boss that she'll be taking over our account for the next month, and he just screamed at me for an hour. You'd better have a good explanation."

If ever there was a time for Ty's innate charm and good looks to work their magic, it was now. Ty turned from the window and in an instant, Rachel's demeanor changed. She no longer wanted Julie's ass on a platter. She was obviously envisioning a gorgeous NFL superstar in her bed, instead.

"I'd like to introduce you to Ty Calhoun, my newest client."

Julie usually appreciated her own curves. But standing this close to a stick-thin woman who could have been ruling the catwalk in Milan rather than working on political campaigns was more than a little depressing. Ty would naturally want to sleep with Rachel—what man wouldn't?

Though it was ridiculous to even think that way —she had no claim on Ty and she didn't want one. She *didn't*.

Ty was all charm as he shook Rachel's hand and steered her over to Julie's leather couch.

"Nice to meet you," he said, and Julie thought the woman was going to climax right then and there. "Julie's told me so much about you," he lied, and she shot him a huge look of thanks.

Rachel was strangely mute. It was comforting to know that all women lost their minds around Ty.

"I'm afraid there's been a huge misunderstanding," he continued. "And I'd hate for anyone to blame Julie or her firm for assigning another consultant to your project."

Julie held back a grin as she watched Rachel actively work to pull herself together. No wonder Ty got away with everything; he was irresistible. It was in his DNA.

"I'd be happy to speak with your boss if that will help you out," he offered.

Flirtatiously, Rachel put her hand on his arm. "Would you really? I know what a big fan he is of yours. Maybe we could meet him for dinner and then slip away for a private drink."

Julie almost gagged. She couldn't listen to another second of this nonsense. If the two of them wanted to fuck like bunnies, fine, but not in her office.

She grabbed her leather bag off the floor and shoved several files into it. "Well, I'm so glad you two have met, but I'm afraid Ty and I have a lot of work to do, as you might imagine. And his evenings are completely full for the next two weeks."

Ty walked Rachel out of the office and back into the front reception area. Julie trailed behind. "I'll be looking forward to our drink," Rachel called as she floated out of the front door.

"She's off-limits," Julie warned. "If you leave her high and dry she'll blame me and pull her business."

They headed into the parking lot. "Don't worry. She's not my type."

There he went again. "When will you get it through your thick skull that I'm not interested in you, other than as a client?"

"When you stop acting like you are."

His low, soft voice hit her in all the places she'd been trying to hide from him.

"Don't think I've forgotten, Julie. You owe me a kiss. That was the bargain."

Her heart sped up. "Fine. Let's get it over with," she said as if she couldn't have cared less.

Just barely, she resisted the urge to purse her lips together and peck him on the cheek like a two-year-old. Even she knew that wasn't the deal they'd made back in her office when Rachel came barreling in.

"Come here," he said, and she wanted him to kiss her more than she'd ever wanted something before.

"Not here. Not in the parking lot."

"Right here. In the parking lot." His eyes held hers. "Now."

She couldn't argue with him. Not when this was his kiss to claim. The thing was, they hadn't really kissed in his underground lair. Yes, he'd made her come, but there had been a challenge behind it, a game of dominance.

This was going to be their first real kiss in ten years. And Julie knew there wasn't a damn thing she could do to prepare herself for the way it was bound to make her feel.

She walked slowly over to her car where he was standing. When she was within arm's reach he held out his hand, and she didn't know what else to do but let him pull her close. One hand circled her rib cage, the other softly caressed her nape, gently cupping the back of her head.

"You have a great mouth," he said, and the unexpected compliment surprised her so much that she forgot to keep her guard up when he moved his lips down to hers.

She felt his breath and closed her eyes. And then, oh God, his lips touched hers and all she wanted was to taste him. To have him taste her. His lips were warm and soft and perfect, and before she knew what she was doing, her tongue was in his mouth and her hands were in his hair and she was pulling him closer. She wanted *more* than just one kiss, so much more.

He sucked at the sensitive flesh of her lower lip, making shivers run down her spine. His erection pressed into her belly and she pressed against it, wanting more, so much more.

This one simple kiss had turned into a full-blown addiction.

Suddenly, ruthlessly, she dragged her mouth away

from his, pushed against his chest, and unsteadily backed up.

What could she say to make him think his kiss hadn't meant as much to her as it obviously had? She had to say something he couldn't argue with. Otherwise, she had a feeling he'd argue her right into bed.

"I have a date tonight," she declared as she unlocked the car. Thankfully, it was true. How embarrassing it would have been if she'd had to make up a phantom date to seem like she wasn't a total loser.

"Great," he said, looking like he kissed women into delirium all day long without a second thought. "Looking forward to it."

Her keys missed the ignition by a mile.

"Are you crazy? You're not coming on my date!" Then she remembered that she'd told Bobby she wouldn't let Ty out of her sight. "Oh God. Of course you are."

He leaned back against the passenger seat. "I'm sure I could find some other way to entertain myself while you're gone."

Julie started the car. "Oh, I think going on my date tonight will be entertainment enough," she said darkly.

✳

Ty was very pleased about moving into Julie's little house at the top of Noe Valley for the next couple weeks. But tagging along with her on a date was a bit much—especially since he already wanted to pound the unknown guy's head into the ground.

He lounged on her couch and flipped through the channels. She'd muttered something about needing to get some work done, threatened him with, "Don't you dare to even open my front door or I'll hunt you down and kill you with my bare hands and maybe a sharp knife," then disappeared into her home office. He'd made some calls to his friends to let them know he was going to be busy for a while with some business stuff, chatted with his agent about the pretty public picture he was going to create for Bobby and the Outlaws, then got bored.

And lonely.

Ty couldn't think of the last time he'd had more than fifteen minutes to himself. His house was a constant scene. The party from the night before continued by the pool the next day in an endless cycle. And until yesterday, he hadn't been down into his sanctum for months.

Silence made him restless. When he was with other people he could just sit and listen to them talk. It was easy to live up to their expectations of him. It wasn't quite as easy to figure out what his own expectations were, so he'd quit trying. But for some reason, he cared about what Julie thought. He wanted to show her she was wrong about him.

He turned the TV off and wandered over to a book case. Why should he care if she thought he was a worthwhile human being? He made a lot of money for a lot of people—the Outlaws, his agent. He gave more money away than anyone would ever guess to charity, to friends in need, and through the team.

But he was pretty sure Julie already knew all that, and wasn't impressed. She didn't think he was capable of being a gentleman.

He sneered at the word as he picked up a weathered copy of *The Great Gatsby*, one of his favorite books. Then he lay down across her couch, his legs hanging over the end. Girly couches and pro football players were rarely a good fit. This one was pretty damn comfortable, even though it could have used three more feet in length.

He was heading into the story's climax a couple hours later when he looked up and realized Julie was standing in the doorway. Actually, she was staring at the book in his hand. She probably didn't think he could read, that the books in his underground den were merely stage props.

But he couldn't work up any indignation. Not when she looked so damn good.

"Is that what you're wearing?"

She pulled her gaze away from the book, ran her

fingers through her soft blonde waves, then pushed her shoulders back.

"No, this is what I throw on to make a sandwich. I'll get dressed for my date later."

Ty was too busy looking at her to pay attention to her sarcastic remark.

Fuck, she was gorgeous. The little red lacy thing she was wearing gave the impression of being see-through. It was the kind of dress that guys would be staring at all night to see if they could maybe, just maybe, see something they weren't supposed to.

Yet she didn't look at all trashy; far from it. Julie couldn't pull off slutty if someone held a gun to her head. On her a strapless red dress and fuck-me heels were sexy yet classy.

"You look amazing."

Her big blue eyes flashed surprise and Ty realized that he liked surprising her. A lot. He'd finally done something to make her feel good, rather than angry and irritated with him.

"I hope this guy is worth it."

So much for the nice moment, he thought as she spun around and went into the kitchen. He followed her in and opened her fridge.

"Make yourself at home," she said, full of snark again.

"Might as well," he said as he moved bottles

of organic juice around. "You got anything in here that might not get me labeled 'pussy' on the playground?"

"I don't drink," she said, prim as a nun.

A new fantasy immediately popped into his head. Once he got her into his bed, maybe he could convince her to play the highly-fuckable-nun-who-has-decided-to-make-a-break-from-everything-she-knows-in-an-indecent-red-dress-and-stiletto-heels role. Now *there* was some nice imagery. Very nice.

"You shouldn't, either," she added as his cock got harder beneath the zipper of his jeans. It took him several seconds to figure out what she was talking about. "Since your body is your job and all, I can't see how alcohol helps."

He grabbed a bottle of organic carrot juice, unscrewed the top, then drank straight from the bottle. A look of distaste crossed her face. She really was too easy.

He took the now-empty container over to the sink and rinsed it out. "I agree with you."

That made her pause. "Then why do you drink?"

"I don't."

Ah, there was that surprise again.

"You actually expect me to believe that you go to strip clubs sober?" She shook her head. "You're nuts."

She didn't need to know that he'd stopped drinking ten years ago. The morning she'd walked away and never turned back.

"My father was a drunk."

She nodded. "I know. But I guess I thought . . ."

The doorbell rang, and all the things Ty wanted to say were lost in his sudden rage at the asshole on the other side of the door who thought he could touch Julie.

For the next two weeks, Julie was off limits.

To everyone except *him*.

CHAPTER TWELVE

There were many reasons why this date-plus-one should have been mortifying: The fact that Ty got to meet a guy she'd liked enough to have dinner with; that she had to explain to Dave that Ty was accompaning them to the restaurant for business reasons; that the owner of the packed restaurant had no trouble whatsoever finding a larger table for "the great Ty Calhoun and his friends" even though there was a two-hour-wait out on the sidewalk; and that Dave was quite possibly the world's biggest Outlaw fan and knew every significant play Ty had made since college, seemed to have memorized their playbook, and hadn't so much as looked at Julie after she'd opened the door.

But the most mortifying thing of all was that Ty clearly felt so sorry for her that he kept coming to her rescue.

For the past hour she'd counted bites, then chews, then sips of water, because even those were more interesting than Dave's incessant football chatter.

Finally, Ty cut him off. "Did you know Julie and I went to high school together?"

Uh-oh.

Dave's mouth opened, making him look like a fish on a hook. What had she ever seen in him?

"Oh man, I can't believe you actually witnessed Ty's moves when he was a teenager. That must have been awesome."

She shook her head. "I didn't go to any football games."

Dave's big mouth grew impossibly bigger. "You missed watching one of the greatest high school players of all time in action? What were you thinking?"

What a total jerk. "Do you really want to know what I was thinking, Dave? Or would you rather ask Ty instead?" she asked sweetly.

Dave blinked in confusion. "Okay." He turned to Ty. "Why didn't she go to football games?"

Ty looked impossibly handsome in the dim light, and Julie was sure every woman in the restaurant was having an orgasm over him. She didn't know how he did it, let all those people stare at him, probe at him. She liked her privacy and couldn't imagine giving it up.

"Julie hates football," Ty told Dave.

"Are you crazy?" he squeaked, a very unattractive sound from a man.

Ty answered for her. "Not everyone likes sports. You've got to respect the fact that people are different, that they have their own interests." Ty turned away from the bumbling fool. "Who is your favorite novelist, Julie?"

Something within her sparked into life. "Alive or dead?"

"Dead."

"Jane Austen."

"Painter. Dead."

"Mary Cassat."

"Musician. Dead."

"Johnny Cash."

He laughed. "Really?"

She shrugged, smiling for the first time all night. "I've always been a sucker for a rebel."

Who would have thought Ty could be so nice? That he'd actually care about her interests, that he wouldn't hold it against her that she didn't know what a safety was?

Clearly, though, Dave didn't care for the new topic of conversation. "What are your plans for next season, Ty?"

Ty waved over the waiter. "I think we're done here. Thanks." He handed him a credit card.

Turning to her loser of a date, he said, "First, I'm going to get to bed early tonight."

Dave nodded, happy to bask in the glow of his hero, not realizing that his moment of glory had just come to an end.

The waiter quickly returned and Ty signed the bill, then held out a hand to Julie. She gladly accepted it and let him pull her toward him.

He whispered, "Say good night, be nice, and whatever you do, *don't* invite him back to your house."

His words were soft and comforting, rather than bossy.

Dave followed at Ty's heels like a puppy dog following its master. Forcing herself to be polite, Julie smiled and said, "It's been a lovely evening, Dave, but I'm afraid I've got an early day ahead of me tomorrow. Good night."

Not surprisingly, he barely blinked in her direction. "Fine. Great. So, Ty, you up for getting a beer? I could call some friends to meet us."

A muscle jumped in Ty's cheek and his voice turned cold. "Sorry to disappoint, buddy, but I've got a beautiful woman waiting for me to take her home."

Julie's heart pounded. She didn't need Ty to be her knight in shining armor. Yet it felt so good to hear him call her beautiful.

Dave shook his head admiringly. "Wow, you must get all the babes. Who is she?"

A sneer curled Ty's lips and Julie was taken aback, accustomed to the carefree grin that drove everyone wild.

"We're keeping our relationship under wraps," he said. "She's not convinced I'm good enough for her yet."

As Dave's mouth dropped open again, Ty put his big palm on the small of Julie's back and guided her through the front door, then out around the corner.

Perfectly happy to go wherever Ty was leading her if it meant getting away from that über-jerk, she was surprised to find that he'd just steered her into a tiny pizza joint.

"Two slices with everything on 'em and a pitcher of Coke," he told a passing waiter, then pushed her into a carved wooden booth and shoved in next to her. "Please tell me that was a blind date."

Her stomach was grumbling. The waiter slid two enormous pizza slices onto the table. She picked one up and inhaled.

"I wish." She took a bite. And then another. "God, this is good."

Julie couldn't deny how nice it was to have Ty's warm, hard body pressed up against her in the little booth. He was watching her eat, his eyes moving from her mouth, to her throat, to the tops of her breasts on display in her red dress.

She felt like an idiot for even bothering to dress

up for a dud like Dave, but at the same time, part of her was happy she'd looked good. Foolishly, she liked it when Ty looked at her. Liked it even better when he was enticed by what he saw.

She looked down at her empty plate, then at his full one. She'd been raised always to be a lady. And a lady never ate more than a man, never raised her voice, never put herself in an untenable position.

Thus far with Ty, Julie had done all three. And the strangest thing was, she wasn't the least bit ashamed of any of it. In fact, she felt downright good.

"You gonna eat that?" she asked, swiping his slice before he could answer.

"Few things are sexier than a woman who eats," Ty murmured, and his words felt like a caress. Her nipples hardened beneath the thin fabric of her dress.

She gulped down some soda, then wiped her mouth off with the back of her hand. God, she loved how free she suddenly felt.

"I refuse to believe that any of those women by your pool eat. They're all ribs and silicone."

He stared at her. "I don't believe I've ever called those girls sexy, have I?"

She forced herself to swallow. "I guess I just assumed."

"They're not my type."

The noise of the pizza joint fell away and she felt like they were the only people in the room.

"As far back as I can remember, I've had a thing for curvy blondes with big . . ."

Why did he have to be so predictable, such a cavemen?

"Brains." He grinned, then looked down at her amply presented chest. "Although a nice pair of breasts is good too."

She reached out for her soda, trying not to show how pleased she was by his comment. "We all know you're a master at coming on to women," she said, trying to extricate herself from the position she was in. The one where she was about to beg him to take her right then, right there on the table. "Unexpected compliments, focusing on their hidden assets."

Ignoring her sarcasm, he said, "I just want to say one more thing about tonight, and I don't want you to try to turn it around or read anything bad into it, okay?"

She looked up at him and saw sincerity in his eyes. "I'm all ears."

"Your date was an ass. He was crazy for not paying attention to you. And he doesn't deserve you."

His words hung in the air, and Julie could have sworn she heard what he didn't say: *And I don't deserve you, either.*

Only she was starting to wonder if maybe he did.

Ty bought her an ice cream cone and she enjoyed

it more than she should have. If she'd had any sense of self-preservation she would have ended the night long ago, locked herself in her bedroom and forced herself to watch the news or read a book.

But surprisingly, she enjoyed his company. He had a natural charm with his fans. Dozens of people wanted pictures and autographs outside the ice cream parlor. When the two of them finally returned to her home, everything in her world felt like it had been turned upside down.

She couldn't deny the truth any longer. She wanted him. Desperately. Wanted him touching her, kissing her. Wanted him inside her. Her body no longer cared what her brain was telling it or the warning sirens clanging around in her head.

"Thanks for a great night," she said, and she meant it. But she also hoped that he'd know she was trying to say she didn't want it to end.

He reached for her hands, rubbed his thumbs across the sensitive skin. "How about next time we leave your date at home?"

"Okay," she whispered, letting him pull her closer. She hadn't wanted to be kissed this much since she was eighteen, when she saw Ty walking across the deck straight toward her, the embodiment of her crush.

"Good night, Julie," he said, then leaned down and kissed her gently on the cheek.

She stood completely still, her heart sinking like a rock. She watched him walk down the hall into her guest bedroom and close the door with a soft click.

She'd just been turned down by the one man who had never turned down anyone in his life. She'd never felt so stupid, so embarrassed, so senselessly aroused in all her life.

∗

Ty sat down hard on the queen-size bed in the guest room. His hands were shaking. Did Julie have any idea how fucking hard it was for him to keep his hands off of her? How much he wanted to take her right there on the carpet in front of her fireplace?

He couldn't think of the last time he'd been this hard. Blue balls were not something he experienced on a regular basis—until Julie.

Of all the times to decide to act like a goddamned gentleman.

Ty ripped off his shirt, breaking several buttons in his haste. He wanted Julie to know that he could behave appropriately, that he respected her, that he wasn't going to ravage her without wooing her first.

Not that pizza and ice cream were the most romantic things in the world, but they were a hell of a lot better than a boring dinner with the world's most boring guy.

Jeez, what on earth had she seen in that jerk?

It was obvious from looking at the guy that he was wealthy and successful and came from the right side of the tracks. But apart from that, he didn't have anything going for him. Julie could do much better. Didn't she know that?

He turned on ESPN and hit the floor to do some sit-ups.

He hoped Julie was happy with the sacrifice he made in the name of honor tonight. Because he wasn't sure he had it in him to be a gentleman again.

*

She rolled over on her stomach, then her left side, then her right. She counted to a hundred, then counted back to one, but nothing helped. She couldn't sleep—not with Ty so near. For hours she'd stared at the wall, wished she had X-ray vision, wished she could see what he was wearing, if he was naked. Was he touching himself, was he pretending her lips were on him, her hands?

Again she heard a voice inside her say, Enough! *But this time, it wasn't telling her to stop falling for the one man she'd sworn never to have feelings for again. No, this time it said,* Go get what you want, what you need. Go on. Go now.

She ripped off her sleep shirt and dug in her lingerie drawer for something lacy. Then she walked out into the hall, to Ty's closed door.

Don't think, *the voice urged,* just open it.

Slowly, she turned the knob and crept into his room. Moonlight streamed in the bay window, illuminating his perfect form reclined on the bed.

"What took you so long?"

His question was softly sensuous and she instinctively moved toward him.

"I wanted to make you wait," she said, not recognizing her own voice.

"I'm not a patient man," he said, and she smiled.

"Too bad. Tonight we're playing by my rules."

He was lying on his back, his hands propping up his head. "Next time we'll play by mine."

She pulled the sash from her robe and moved slowly to the bed. His magnificent chest was bare and she couldn't resist toying with him, dragging the edge of the pink sash across his tanned expanse of skin.

He growled deep from his chest and reached for her.

She took a step back. "Somehow I didn't think I could trust you to behave yourself. Keep your arms above your head."

His brown eyes followed her as she moved up to the head of the bed. Her open robe revealed a short, tight, and translucent slip.

He hadn't obeyed her command yet, so she threatened, "I can either use this on your eyes or your wrists. Your choice."

A wicked, aroused smile curved his lips. "What if I choose one now, one later?"

"My rules, Ty. Make your choice."

She never knew how much she liked being in charge, liked playing the bad girl.

Being with a bad boy like Ty had roused her inner seductress.

"Wrists," he said. "But first, this." He reached up and pulled her slip off over her head, leaving her naked but not the least bit chilled. Everywhere he looked, every place his fingers drifted, was burning up.

Knowing it would drive him crazy, she leaned over him as she tied his arms to the bedpost with the sash. Her breasts swayed over his mouth and she was sorely tempted to drop her nipples into his waiting mouth. But she wanted to tease him, to tantalize him, wanted him to burst with desire for her before she gave in.

His wrists secure, she pulled down the sheets that covered him.

He was blessedly naked. And so incredibly beautiful.

His cock rose up, huge and thick. "I take it you found what you were looking for?"

His words were taunting and yet seductive.

"I can't stop reliving what you did to me yesterday with your hands, your mouth. I can't stop thinking about what it would have been like if the tables had been turned."

He swallowed hard. "Turn them."

She climbed up on the bed and straddled his thighs. "I can't help but wonder if you taste as good as you look."

His voice was strangled. "There's only one way to find out."

She smiled. "Who says jocks aren't smart?"

Slowly leaning down, letting her hair brush against his abdominal muscles so that they jumped and tightened, she pressed her lips to the tip of his cock. A drop of liquid surfaced and she licked it off in one smooth stroke. Until this moment, Julie had never been a big fan of blow jobs.

Funny how one man could change her opinion about absolutely everything.

She ran her tongue lightly down the long, thick shaft. How had they managed to fit together when she was an eighteen-year-old virgin?

She couldn't wait to find out again.

Without warning, she took him deep into her mouth.

His hips bucked up off the bed and he groaned her name. She loved watching him lose control, loved knowing that she was the woman making it happen.

"Untie me," he growled.

She shook her head. "Not until I'm done with you."

As much as she loved tasting him, giving him pleasure with her tongue and lips, she wanted to feel him deep within her more. Right now.

She moved up his body, put her hands on his chest, and pushed down onto his cock, letting his first thick inch spread her wide open. She'd relived their lovemaking so many times over the past ten years, yet nothing could have possibly lived up to the incredible reality.

"More, Julie. Take more," he urged and she gave in, taking him in another inch. Before she could stop herself, before she could remember to slow down to torture him with longing, she slid all the way down, pressed her pelvic bone against his.

And that was when Julie realized she'd been lying to herself: Having any control over her body where Ty was concerned was impossible. All she wanted was him inside her just like this, hard and pulsing. She couldn't get enough of him, never wanted this bliss to end.

"Untie me," he said again, somewhere between an order and a plea. But before she got the chance, his arm muscles rippled and the fabric ripped in two. Then his hands were on her, and they were everywhere—her breasts, her clitoris, her bottom . . . an orgasm began to ripple across her breasts, over her stomach, deep in her core.

Julie panted, her hand between her legs, Ty's name on her lips as she came. The sheets were twisted around her, and it took her several moments to realize that she wasn't in her guest bedroom. She was in her own bedroom.

And Ty was still on the other side of the wall.

CHAPTER THIRTEEN

Julie woke up curled tightly around her extra pillow. Her eyes felt gritty and puffy; the light seemed harsher than usual.

Oh, Lord—while he slept peacefully a bedroom away, she'd been in the throes of a wet dream that had seemed utterly real.

Well. She'd never get through this assignment without a serious dose of positive thinking, so from now on, she'd keep her emotions firmly in check and her mind on the business at hand.

Jay, Ty's agent, had filled her in on the rest of Ty's off-season schedule yesterday afternoon during a phone meeting, and tonight she and Ty were attending an important charity event in the vineyards of Napa Valley.

She sat up and reached for her watch, then glanced at the time. 10:00 A.M.?

She blinked hard and looked again. Her internal body clock always woke her up at 6:30 A.M., even when she changed time zones!

How could this have happened?

Ty shook everything up. *Everything*.

She jumped in the shower, dried her hair, did her makeup, and dressed in record time. Then she headed for the kitchen, looking for coffee, hoping Ty was engrossed in TV or something.

No such luck.

He looked up from the sunny corner where her round, stone kitchen table was tucked beneath a bank of windows. It looked like he had several contracts spread in front of him and a yellow legal notepad full of scribblings. Great. He was working hard on business matters while she was sleeping away the morning. Yet again, he'd managed to get a leg up on her.

"Looks like you could use some coffee," he said. "I just brewed a fresh pot." As if he could read her mind he added, "I got in the habit of waking up early at training camp in college. Never figured out how to sleep till noon like some of the other guys."

She nodded and poured herself a large steaming cup of coffee, not trusting herself to speak until she'd imbibed a lethal dose of caffeine.

Hell, she barely trusted herself to be in the same room with Ty. If her dream was any indication of her sex-starved state, she was perilously low on self-control.

"I'm usually up early too," she said, feeling defensive and hating it.

He sat back in his chair. "Something keep you awake last night?"

She scowled at his low blow. Grabbing a banana from the fruit bowl on the kitchen island, she sat in the chair across the table from temptation.

"I had to take some work to bed," she replied. When she realized exactly how she'd *taken her work to bed,* she blushed profusely. Crap! She never blushed. As a fair-skinned blonde she'd had to teach herself early not to reveal her emotions so easily. Whether in personal or professional situations, keeping her control was vitally important.

"Mmm-hmm," he said.

Was she imagining the slightly mocking note in his voice? Or was she just feeling guilty?

As if the earth's rotation depended on it, she cracked open the top of the banana, peeled one long slice down to the bottom, then the next. Finally the firm, yellow flesh was ready for her to eat.

Just as she was bringing the pointy tip to her lips, she looked up at Ty. His eyes were trained on her mouth, on the banana she had clasped in her hand.

Oh God, how had breakfast become so incredibly mortifying?

Her first instinct was to drop the banana. But something inside her wanted to punish Ty for taunting her in her dreams last night. She'd never felt like this before, so constantly tempted and on the verge of doing bad things.

She slowly brought the banana to her lips. Covering the tip with her mouth, she sucked in an inch, and then another, finally taking a slow bite, closing her eyes in pleasure as she chewed.

She heard Ty's coffee cup hit the table with a clatter, and she smiled. She felt much better when they were on an even playing field.

"Our first event is tonight," she said. "In Napa."

He shifted in his seat. "Don't wear that little red dress again."

"Excuse me?" she said sharply, even though she would never wear something so sexy to a work function. Last night was the first time she'd ever worn the impulse buy; it was far more revealing than her usual style.

Her mother had always said that men couldn't control themselves, so there was no need to dress like a whore and tempt them to make a pass at her. And while Julie knew that her mother was bitter over the buxom young girls her father made no secret of sleeping with, she'd still taken the advice to heart.

"Don't get me wrong, you looked great in it. Too good. Way too good."

She liked his compliment. Far too much. It was time to put Ty firmly in his place.

"Your team hired *me* to tell *you* what to wear. Not the other way around."

"I get that. But Montague is a dirty old man. You wear that dress and he'll be eyeing your breasts all night, trying to cop a feel when he thinks no one is looking. As it is, he'll be following you around all night like a dog chasing a juicy bone."

"You're the first person who has ever compared me to a dog bone. Now, that's a compliment to remember."

"You're welcome."

He grinned and she couldn't keep herself from grinning back. It was so easy, sitting with him like this in her breakfast nook, even when they were sniping at each other.

She gestured to his papers. "Got some contracts to look over?"

He gathered up the papers. "My agent couriered over some new ad contracts. You wouldn't believe the amount of paperwork I have to deal with."

He was right. She'd believed football players were nothing more than big, dumb guys in tight white pants chasing a ball during hailstorms. She'd never thought of them as businessmen before. Now she knew better.

"Speaking of your agent, he sent over your

appearance schedule. I've already crossed out several inappropriate events."

He stood up, picked up their empty coffee cups, and put them in the sink. She hadn't had the pleasure of seeing him in jeans and a T-shirt until now.

Desire nearly undid her. Annoyed by her reaction, she added, "And I don't care who your dates are supposed to be for the charity events. From this point forward you're going stag, with me just one step behind."

"I'm all yours," he replied in a low, sensual tone, deliberately letting her explore the idea of his really being hers.

Just as she had in her dream last night when she'd tied him up and had her way with him.

"The only thing that's nonnegotiable is football camp," he added.

"I thought training didn't start until July?"

"It doesn't. I volunteer coach at a camp for kids. The best and the brightest."

Julie was surprised, and she said thoughtfully, "It must be like looking in a mirror."

She could have sworn his eyes clouded over. "Sometimes it is."

"There must be so much pressure on those kids," she said, and his eyes met hers. For a second, she saw everything he wanted to keep hidden.

It hit her square in the chest: She wanted to be

close to him. But could she actually risk dropping the walls she'd erected to protect her heart to find out more about what was in Ty's?

"I've got to work out for a couple of hours. I'll grab my stuff so we can head to the gym."

Just as quickly as he'd opened himself to her, he closed off, and she felt oddly alone in her warm and cozy kitchen.

✳

Julie had a knack for hitting too close, Ty thought as he bench-pressed three hundred for ten reps. He was pushing himself, trying to work off some of the relentless energy pushing through him.

Through the glass wall, he could see Julie sitting in the gym's café, talking on her cell phone, taking notes, and tapping on her laptop. She was always so focused, so driven. She didn't smile nearly enough.

She picked up a clear plastic cup with the green sludge the trainers insisted was "power" protein and took a sip. Her face scrunched up and her cheeks sucked in with obvious disgust.

Yet another thing they had in common, he thought as she surreptitiously spit it back into the cup after looking around to make sure no one was looking.

She seemed distracted this morning, and he was

hoping he knew the reason why. All night long he'd been falling in and out of triple X dreams of the two of them. Him on her, her on him. Doggy-style. Up against the wall. Sixty-nine.

In his dreams, he'd had her in every possible way. Was it too much to hope that she wasn't any more immune to him than he was to her?

He got off the bench and picked up an eighty-pound barbell to work on his triceps. How pathetic would he be if he got an erection at the gym? He had to stop acting like a teenage boy dreaming about getting his first piece of ass.

Dominic DiMarco, one of the veteran Outlaws, walked into the gym, and Ty watched him speak to Julie. When Julie laughed, jealousy drop-kicked Ty.

Dominic was one of the few guys on the team who went home alone after a game, who didn't burn it out with groupies hanging on to him. A girl like Julie was probably just what Dominic was looking for, the perfect gorgeous, smart woman to settle down with.

Whereas Ty was fucking around and wasting his time.

His triceps burned as he pumped the weight harder in jealousy and frustration.

Dominic dropped his gym bag on the floor between them and picked up some weights. "Julie's with you?"

Fuck. They were already on a first-name basis.

"I'm living with her," Ty said, then felt like an idiot for trying to lay claim to her before his friend could. He'd never acted like such a pussy before.

Dominic laughed. "Sean told me your new image consultant had you on a short leash." He did a curl, then winced in pain. "Good time to be a dog, I'd say." Then he asked, "You like being with her?"

Ty grunted as he did his last rep. "Sure," he said in an offhand way. Time to change the subject. "Your shoulder still giving you trouble?"

Dominic dropped to a lower weight. "A little," he admitted. "Julie said you knew each other in high school. Pretty girl."

Ty could think of a hundred better words to describe her than pretty.

"Thinking of settling down?" Dominic asked.

Ty forced a laugh. "No way. Not with all the action I get." It sounded empty, even to himself.

"I know you're not asking for my advice," Dominic said, putting down his weights and pinning Ty with a glance in the mirror. "Hell, you probably don't even need it. Forget I said anything."

Ty sat down on the incline bench, figuring it wouldn't hurt to let Dominic say his piece.

"I'm listening."

"I made some bad decisions way back." Dominic shook his head.

Ty nodded, wondering where Dominic was heading with this. He'd never been much for other people's opinions, but Dominic had the years, the experience behind him to back up whatever he was going to say.

"If you're lucky enough to meet someone special, don't let her go. You've got money and fame already. But you won't have her."

CHAPTER FOURTEEN

Later that afternoon, during the ninety-minute drive from San Francisco to Napa, Julie couldn't dismiss the feeling that something had changed. For some reason, Ty was going out of his way to be nice. Attentive. Even sweet.

She knew he desired her. And the clearer he made that, the less immune she was to it.

Already, she was worrying about making it home fully dressed. And if she could barely keep her panties on during a ninety-minute car ride, how could she possibly last the next eleven days? With every passing hour, Ty was making it clearer and clearer that he wanted to be with her, sleep with her, give her pleasure.

If only she could trust him not to turn around and break her heart again.

Fortunately, Ty misinterpreted her quietness.

"Are you afraid I'm going to act up at the party? Get all the woman to rip off their clothes and jump naked into the fountain?"

She took in the sharp planes of his cheeks, his strong nose, full mouth. Those dark brown eyes that knocked her right in the gut.

Surprisingly, what she saw in them reassured her. For some reason that she didn't understand, he was going to try to behave.

"Would it hurt your feelings if I said no?"

He kept his gaze on hers. "Don't worry. I'll make up for it later."

Instinctively she smiled. "I have no doubt that you will."

At last they pulled up in front of the vineyard estate. Ty held out his hand to help her out of the car, his heat enveloping her. As the limo pulled away, they stood together on the golden pavers, her hand still in his.

"Have I told you how beautiful you are?"

"Thank you."

"I'm not just talking about tonight."

No. He couldn't say something like that to her when her resistance was so low. She couldn't afford to let his admiration sink in.

"You clean up pretty good yourself. I like the suit."

"I'll tell them to blame you."

She cocked her head to one side. "Why?"

"They're paying for flash and trash. I usually put on my diamond-studded grill for events like this."

She frowned. "You do not." Then, when he didn't say anything, "*Do* you?"

He laughed. "You're too easy."

Their host suddenly appeared beside the Tuscan-inspired fountain at the top of the steps.

"There he is, the man of the hour. Ty Calhoun. And of course, a beautiful woman on his arm."

As Gordon Montague made his approach down the steps, Julie tried to pull away from Ty. She wasn't his date, she was his employee. She'd stay just close enough to keep an eye on him.

But he refused to let her go. Instead, he put his hand on the small of her back. Exactly where his hand always seemed to be.

"Gordon Montague at your service." Their host lifted her hand to his lips in a gesture that should have seemed gallant, but came across as creepy instead.

Julie fought the urge to roll her eyes. "Thank you for allowing me to accompany Ty to your party."

Gordon turned to the devastating man beside her. "Even a superstar like you pales in comparison to your companion's ravishing beauty."

"Hey, Monty," Ty said, pulling Gordon's tight grasp off her hand under the pretense of shaking it. "How goes it? What's on the agenda for tonight?"

He was doing it again. Always coming to her rescue.

"We're fund-raising for leukemia tonight." He turned to Julie. "My wife's sister's friend was touched by the disease."

Feigned concern did not suit Gordon in the least.

Ty grinned. "I'm always up for a dog and pony show for a good cause. Who would you like me to meet first?"

Ty was so irreverent, not the least bit bowled over by Gordon's money, his connections, his power. She'd grown up in this world, yet she'd never learned how not to take it seriously. She could learn something from him.

Gordon led them inside, and as the evening progressed from cocktails and appetizers to a seven-course sit-down dinner paired with expensive wines, it became abundantly clear that no one knew quite what to make of her. Was she Ty's girlfriend? His business associate? A groupie?

Julie didn't want to make Ty look bad by saying, "I was hired to watch over him," but she didn't want people to think she was the latest in a long string of one-night-stands, either. She settled for pleasant, but distant when answering curious questions. She enjoyed herself, but not too much. She stood near Ty at all times, but not too close.

Out of the blue, a lovely woman who seemed out of place in a light blue linen dress and shawl pulled Ty aside.

"I'm Gordon's sister, Gina the black sheep of the family. You must be the prized pig."

Ty didn't take offense, just shook her hand and said it was nice to meet her.

"I'm afraid I can't stand too close to you for too long, though. When a man is as good-looking as you, it's dangerous to give anyone the chance to make comparisons." Gina gestured in Julie's direction. "Although I do have to say that the two of you look good together."

Ty turned to Julie. "I told you so." Then to Gina, he added, "She refuses to believe me."

Julie bared her teeth at him, hoping it looked at least a little bit like a smile. "That's because I've never heard so many people use the word 'pretty' to describe a man before."

Gina grinned. "Mark my words, this is the girl for you. She's not blinded by all of your shimmer and shine."

Julie felt completely transparent. She couldn't pinpoint the exact moment that Ty started to get to her; all she knew was that he had, and was doing it still.

And she couldn't let him. No matter what.

"Excsue me, I need to find the ladies' room."

She dashed through the lavish ballroom, searching for a place to hide out for a few minutes, to try to regain her equilibrium. She ran into the kitchen, where she saw a set of stairs, a narrow, dark flight that she hoped led up to maids' quarters.

The stairs seemed to go up and up forever, growing darker with every step, climbing up to a secret tower. Something told her to turn back, that she shouldn't be trespassing in a stranger's house, but she was more afraid of the devastatingly handsome man who awaited her at the bottom of the stairs than she was of being caught.

Continuing to climb, she felt for a light switch along the wall. She heard footsteps on the steps behind her a moment before she flicked the switch and gasped aloud.

At the top of Gordon Montague's secret tower was a fully equipped sexual hideaway . . . the last place on earth she wanted Ty to find her.

Only, judging by the heat she felt at her back, he already had.

CHAPTER FIFTEEN

Ty had long believed in the power of positive thinking. Coach after coach during the past decade had pressed the power of visualization upon him and his teammates. Although he wasn't big on woo-woo stuff, acting like you already had what you wanted worked most of the time on the field.

Ty wanted to win games; he won them. He wanted lots of money; he had it. It hadn't occurred to him to use this technique for getting a girl, but then, he'd never wanted anyone nearly as much as he wanted Julie. And he'd certainly never had to work for it like this before, either.

He'd made his way through the kitchen, signed a few autographs, and asked which way she went. Something about the dark stairwell conjured up a flow of sexy images. Julie asking him to unzip her dress, beckoning him over, ripping his clothes off, lying across his lap, begging him to spank her sexy lace-clad ass.

He'd been stuck on this fantastic image as he made his way up the circular stairs. A light scent of apples and cinnamon lingered in the air and he'd known he was on the right track. His cock had hardened at the thought of how soft her ass cheeks would feel beneath his palm, at how good it would feel to cup her breasts with his other hand.

And then she'd switched on the light, and he'd seen a sex toy wonderland. He'd never seen so many erotic pictures, paintings, sculptures, dildos, vibrators, and books outside of a porn shop.

He was clearly better at this ask and you shall receive stuff than he'd ever realized. Maybe when he retired from the game, he'd write a book on visualization.

He whistled at the S and M equipment hanging from the walls, the thick chains by the bed. "Damn. This is some room." He figured Julie was probably freaking out right now.

She giggled. "You know when you took me into your basement? I thought you had one of these rooms under there."

He smiled. "As if I'd ever need to chain a woman down."

Her eyes were big as she examined a two-headed dildo from a distance. He was pretty sure she had no idea what it was for.

"True," she agreed. "But you still could have been into kinky stuff."

He pushed her farther into the room. "Go ahead, examine everything. I know you're dying to."

She made a face. "I'm too grossed out right now. Just thinking about Gordon in here with . . . whoever he comes here with." Her shoulder nearly brushed into a fully erect statue and she jumped. "I hope he washes everything on a regular basis."

As Ty did a quick perusal of the room's contents, he could see Julie warring with herself, opening her mouth, then shutting it.

"Go ahead, ask me. I know you're dying to."

She stood in the center of the room, a perfect, pure goddess in the midst of sin. "Have you ever . . ." Her cheeks flushed pink.

"Once."

Her mouth flew open. "You've used this stuff?"

He grinned, looked around at the impressive contraptions. He wasn't into anything crazy, but a pair of handcuffs with Julie certainly wouldn't suck.

"Not exactly."

"Please tell me pictures aren't going to surface of you naked in leather chaps with a spiked collar around your neck."

"I went to an S and M club once, a long time ago. Just to watch. Not participate." He shrugged. "Every guy wonders."

"Not the guys I know," she muttered. Then she asked, "Was it weird? Or . . ." She looked like she couldn't quite get her mouth around the word. "Exciting?"

Ty spotted a balcony out the window, and he grabbed her hand.

"Come outside with me and I'll tell you," he said as she willingly escaped with him out a set of French doors.

The view from the rooftop terrace was breathtaking. The sun was just starting to set over endless fields of vines, and the air was scented with growing grapes. Holding Julie's hand, something in Ty's chest buzzed like he was on the verge of a game-winning play.

"Honestly," he said as he rubbed his thumb softly against her palm, "I don't need a bunch of contraptions and semi-naked strangers to make sex exciting."

She looked up at him, her blue eyes almost translucent in the sunset's reflection.

He was going to put himself out on the line. He'd just have to pray that she wouldn't take him down. "All I need is you."

＊

It should have sounded like a sappy come-on but it didn't. And there were a million things she could have said, like, *"I bet you say that to all the girls,"* or *"Give me one reason to believe you."* But she didn't.

The only words she had were, "One night only."

He stared at her with an intensity that made her go hot all over.

"Only tonight."

He moved quickly, not giving her a chance to change her mind, to listen to the part of her brain that was reminding her she was on the clock right now, that she was supposed to be policing Ty's licentious activities, not leading him down the path of sin.

He brought her hand to his lips, kissing the pad of one finger. His lips were soft, so soft, and she wasn't prepared, couldn't have ever walled herself off to the sensation of him unfolding her other fingers, of the kisses he laid on her skin, of the way he was worshipping even the smallest areas of her body.

"So stern tonight," he murmured.

He slowly turned her away from him, and she placed her hands on the balcony railing as he pressed his hips against her bottom.

"But always so perfect. So beautiful."

Julie was helpless to move, to speak, to think as his thumb slid up from the base of her neck to her hairline. She held her breath, waiting for his next move, knowing it was going to be just the right one.

She'd twisted her hair in a tight bun. He gently removed the pins holding back her hair one at a time, letting it fall down around her neck and shoulders. Strong fingers massaged her scalp.

A moan emerged from her throat. The longest tips of her hair brushed against the top of her breasts and she found herself wishing his hands were on her, instead.

"Does that feel good?" he whispered against her hair.

"Mmm-hmm," she whispered back, not wanting him to stop the massage, yet wishing he would just push her skirt up and take her from behind without any more foreplay.

His hands moved across her shoulders, his fingers brushing against her collarbones as he slid her black wrap off her shoulders. It slid against her sensitive skin, down her back, to the floor. Julie had never felt so sexy. She'd never been undressed by a man before; no man had ever taken the time.

Ty brushed her hair to one side and began unclasping and untying the tiny strings behind her neck that held up the top of her dress. The way his fingers brushed against her skin, the fact that every ounce of his attention was focused on her, was unbearably sensual.

The fastenings give way and arousal flooded her from head to toe. No matter how things turned out between them, she'd remember his kindness, his tender touch, for the rest of her life.

"I need you to promise me something," he said.

Somehow she managed to nod.

"Promise me you'll tell me if you want me to stop. No matter what."

Deep within her chest, something full and sweet began to blossom.

"I promise."

An instant later, he cupped her breasts in his big hands. She rubbed against him, pressing herself into his palms, and he stroked her with the tips of his fingers.

"Is this okay?" he said in a low voice.

He already knew the answer, but part of their dance was hearing her say it aloud.

She gasped as his thumb and forefinger found her nipples. Her legs were shaky and she leaned into him, into his huge erection, for support.

"It's perfect."

A breath before his mouth came down on her neck, he said, "You're perfect," and then he was nipping at all the sensitive spots he'd remembered for ten long years. All the while he cupped and stroked and caressed her breasts, which seemed to grow fuller, her nipples harder, with every kiss.

"I want more," he said softly and she pushed her hips into his as a silent "Yes."

In a moment, her dress fell to the terra-cotta tiles.

His gaze roved up her legs, her hips, her back, burning a path of sensual destruction. She hadn't been able to resist putting on her sexiest panties, sheer black lace that revealed most of her bottom. She'd told herself she hadn't worn them with the intention of Ty ever seeing them, but now, as she stood before him gripping tightly to the cool rail, she knew she had.

Every single thing she'd done since he'd re-entered her world had been with the intention of seduction. Every movement, everything she'd said, everything she'd thought, had been about fulfilling temptation.

She wanted him to want her.

And he did.

She wanted pleasure.

And he would give it to her.

She turned her head slightly and he pounced. His mouth claimed hers, and one hand curved around her rib cage to fondle her breasts again. *Please,* she begged silently, *please touch me between my legs.*

Answering her prayers, his free hand began the slow trip past her belly button, under the thin triangle of lace, and found her already wet and slick, ready for everything he would give her before the night was through. His palm cupped her, one finger dipping between her folds. She arched her breasts into one hand, pressed her hips against the other. He tortured her with pleasure, building her desire higher, until she thought she'd scream.

His mouth moved from her lips down to that sensitive spot behind her ear. "Come for me, sweetheart," he whispered and his soft plea pushed her over the peak into an explosive climax. Her muscles clenched around his long, thick finger as an orgasm rocked through her.

She didn't even care if anyone walked outside, looked up, caught them; if anything, the idea excited her.

She turned in his arms, her naked skin brushing against his suit, and reached up to hold his face in her hands.

"I want you naked. Now."

He groaned, and kissed her hard as she slipped her hands under his jacket and pushed it off to fall on top of her dress. She undid the buttons of his crisp, white shirt, and popped his cuff links off, her hands eager to run across the wide, smooth expanse of his chest, over his strong shoulders, down to his hips, then back up his well-muscled back.

"And then," she said, "I want you inside me."

"There *is* a God," he said, then groaned as she pulled his shirt off and pressed a hot kiss to his solar plexus.

"More," she said, undoing his slacks. She wouldn't be satisfied until all of Ty's perfection was laid bare before her.

"Looks like I just have to take care of one last thing," she said, looking at his boxer shorts.

She loved the way his cock was pushing toward her through the thin cotton, loved how close she was to having what she wanted, what she'd literally dreamed of.

"One very *important* thing," Ty said, and she laughed.

Sex and laughter had never been partners in her experience with men; even with Ty on grad night she'd mostly felt awe, fear, excitement, and arousal.

She didn't remember joy bubbling up from an endless fountain.

Still smiling, she gently pulled the waistband of his boxers over his erection. Sweet Lord, he was big.

And oh so beautiful.

Her memory hadn't even come close to the magnificent reality.

Ty's cock was a masterpiece.

She wrapped her fingers around him, sliding her hand up and down the thick, heated length. Ty's thigh muscles tensed.

"Don't get me wrong, honey, what you're doing right now is way up there on my list. But—"

She loosened her grip on his throbbing erection.

As much fun as it would have been to know that she had the power to make him come, she didn't want to lose the chance to take him inside her.

"Please tell me you have a condom on you," she said. If ever there was a time for Ty to live up to his reputation as a lady-killer of epic proportions, it was now. She hadn't brought one, of course, because that would have meant admitting to herself that she intended to have sex with him.

Ty bent down and pulled one out of his inside jacket pocket. In a flash, he'd ripped open the package and slid it onto his shaft.

Looking at the six-plus feet of raw power standing before her, Julie lost her breath. She forgot all about celebrity exposés, forgot about the job she was supposed to be doing tonight, forgot anything but her need to be held by him.

"Here?" he asked. "Against the rail?"

She looked up from his huge, attention-grabbing erection into his eyes.

"Right here."

"Put your arms around my neck," he directed, and she was one step ahead of him, wrapping her legs around his hips too. She loved the way he supported her weight, cupped her flesh in his hands.

"I won't let you fall," he promised.

"I know."

She opened up to him, taking the tip of his dick

inside. She was so wet, so ready for him, in a way that she'd never been for any other man. His muscles tightened as he held her in place on the tip of his shaft. Julie was glad for his endless weight training, his long, hard workouts. No other man could have held her captive like this, on the verge of swallowing him whole.

But Ty could. And she loved it.

"Do you want to hear me beg?" he asked, his words holding an edge she hadn't heard before. Gone was the charming rogue. In its place was the warrior who knew the limits to his restraint and was issuing a sensual warning.

She couldn't be so cruel, so she took him in another inch.

Then all hell broke loose.

His hips pushed into hers, and she couldn't resist taking everything he offered, every last ounce of pleasure. She clung greedily to him as he pushed her back into the balcony's railing and pounded deep into her, then deeper still.

His name was on her lips as she began climbing again, higher and higher, loving the way his dick grew bigger and harder with every stroke.

He used his hands to pivot her hips up and down and rock her clitoris against his pelvic bone. It was good, so good.

"Ty!" she whispered frantically, wanting to scream with pleasure.

"I'm right there with you, sweetheart."

From deep inside her, her climax exploded, her muscles clenching Ty's erection.

His shout was muffled by her hair as he plunged into her one final time, protecting her from the metal railing with his knuckles.

Even through the thick haze of her own orgasm, she loved the way his cock pulsed into her. A part of her mourned the thin separation of the condom between them.

She'd never experienced anything so wonderful in all her life. But as sanity returned, she knew that this one time was all she could risk. No matter how much she yearned otherwise.

CHAPTER SIXTEEN

Julie blew his mind. Every time he touched her, she went off like a rocket.

Besides tonight, there was only one other time he'd reacted so strongly. Back in high school, where Julie had been the hottest thing for miles.

Now he watched her silhouetted against the rising moon, naked and more beautiful than anyone or anything he'd ever seen. An array of emotions moved swiftly across her face.

She didn't think he knew her, but he did. And right about now she was ripe for regret.

Screw regret. Any two people who enjoyed each other as much as they just had owed it to themselves to do it again. And again.

He figured their luck-o-meter on not getting caught was just about running out, so he pushed down the desire to take her again on the chaise lounge ten feet away. Besides, he'd be more convincing in his arguments to keep doing it like bunnies if she thought he was concerned about propriety.

The two of them getting caught, naked, up on the balcony, wouldn't be great for either of their careers.

He bent down to pick up her dress. "Turn around and step into it," he said, holding it up in front of her incredible curves. "I'll zip it up."

She blinked at him a couple of times before following his instructions. She stiffened as his finger moved up her spine, then played at the nape of her neck while he re-did the intricate ties and clasps that held her dress in place.

When she turned back around Ty was caught, yet again, by her incredible beauty. While her dress was oh-so-proper, her hair was wild, pouring sexily over her shoulders. She looked like a well-fucked woman.

"Is my dress ripped? Oh God, we're never going to get away with this are we?" Worry was imprinted between her eyes, around her lips.

"You look great, your dress looks fine, and no one will have a clue about what we've been doing up here," he said as he began putting on his own clothes. Then he grinned. "No one except us."

She moved away but not before he saw her eyes flash with desire, the primal satisfaction that she couldn't hide.

"Speaking of us," she began, and he held out his cuffs to cut her off at the pass.

"Could you help me over here?"

Reflexively she returned to his side and while she was busy putting his cuff links back on, he started spinning.

"You're an incredible lover, Julie," he began and she nearly dropped the Outlaw logo pin she was working on to the floor.

"Please, Ty, let's just pretend this never happened."

"Tell me the truth," he coaxed, hoping he was playing this right. "Do you really want to do that?"

She opened her mouth, almost spoke, then licked her lips. Watching the tip of her tongue move across the sexy curve of her upper lip made him rock hard all over again.

"I'm not going to lie," she said, her voice barely louder than a whisper. "What we just did was great. Really, really great. But we both know we shouldn't do it again. Never, ever again."

Yet something in her voice, in the way her fingers brushed against his wrists as she straightened the edges of his sleeves, made him wonder if she secretly wanted him to talk her into continuing where they'd just left off.

"Okay, now I'll tell you the truth as I see it."

She looked up at him, her blue eyes wide.

"There's fire between us. You and me, we're good together."

She shook her head, pulled away from him, and he reached for her hand. Held her close.

"There's no point in denying it. We have chemistry. And whether we like it or not, I don't think it's going to do either of us any good to try and ignore the sparks between us."

Julie took a deep breath, her eyes trained on their hands. "I just don't see how this could work."

He had to convince her once and for all to throw caution to the wind and have a damn good time with him.

"Look at it this way: We've got almost two weeks together, all day every day. I'm already in your house; you're my date for every event. I think we're both strong enough to enjoy what we want without it screwing ourselves up permanently, don't you?"

He knew she couldn't admit that she wouldn't be able to handle a sex-only relationship with him.

"Maybe," she conceded.

He smiled in anticipation of pleasure to come.

"On one condition," she said.

He nodded, knowing what she was going to say. "No strings attached. That's a given."

Something in her eyes gave him pause, made

him wonder if he should have kept his big mouth shut. Especially since he wasn't even sure he meant what he'd just said.

"Of course there won't be any strings attached," she finally said, waving away his words as if they didn't matter one bit. "But I was going to say that I can only do this if you agree to keep our after-hours relationship completely secret."

He felt like he'd been punched in the gut.

Shit. Why did he care if she didn't want anyone to know they were doing each other? It wasn't like they were dating; they were just going to be having sex. Lots and lots of mind-blowing sex.

Why did he care if all these years later, she was still ashamed of who he was? If she thought he was just a new-money piece of flash who just happened to know how to rock her world?

After all, they were both going to take what they wanted and then go their separate ways.

"I wouldn't have it any other way," he agreed.

Together, silently, they left the balcony, walked back through the sex chamber, and headed back downstairs to the party.

Great, Ty thought. He'd gotten what he wanted.

So why wasn't he happier?

CHAPTER SEVENTEEN

By the time the party wound down, Julie was a basket case.

If she'd thought one taste of perfect love-making would see her through the rest of her days, she was dead wrong. It wouldn't even see her through the evening. She'd been watching the clock all night, desperate to be alone with Ty again. In her house, in her bed, for as long as she pleased.

But what really upset her was the way *"No strings attached. That's a given,"* kept playing over and over in her head like a skipping CD.

"I'm done being a show dog," Ty told her at last, and they went to find their host.

"Had a great time tonight," he said to Gordon. "Thanks for the invite."

"I'm so glad you could be here tonight, Ty. And thank you for bringing your very lovely companion."

Gordon might as well have called her skanky, the way *lovely* sounded coming out of his mouth. Her mind flashed back to his sex room and she barely contained her revulsion.

"I had a wonderful time as well," she said, shaking his dry, bony palm.

"I know you did," he said.

What a weird response.

Ty extricated her hand from Gordon's grasp by leading her toward the front door.

"Most days, I love my job," he said for her ears only.

She nodded, knowing exactly what he was getting at. "Me too."

As Ty alerted his driver via cell phone that they were ready to leave, she looked back up at the house. The tower's balcony, mostly hidden by oak trees, would forever be a wonderful memory.

They slid into the limo and she said, "You were fantastic tonight."

One corner of his mouth quirked up and his eyes gleamed wickedly. "Glad you thought so."

"I was talking about how you interacted with the guests."

"Sure you were."

She laughed, glad she could finally let herself enjoy being with him. Not only was Ty sexy, but he was fun. And surprisingly quick.

She lowered her voice so his driver, Jose, couldn't hear them. "You know how fantastic you were up on the roof."

"Tell me more," he said and she looked pointedly at the front seat.

He pressed a button on the armrest and the glass divider between the front and back seats slid closed. The faint buzz of the talk radio station Jose was listening to disappeared.

"Trust me, he can't hear us."

She shifted as far away from Ty as her seat belt allowed. "I can't . . . do anything. Not while he's still here."

Ty relaxed back into his leather seat and she marveled at how nothing seemed to faze him. Here she was burning up with desire, wondering how she was possibly going to make it through the entire drive home without climbing on Ty's lap and riding him like a cowgirl, and he looked completely relaxed.

"He can't read lips," Ty said.

Her brain was a step behind her hormones. "I don't get it." Then she blushed. "Oh!"

He grinned again, the lazy look of a cat who has already gotten the cream. And wouldn't mind the cherry on top for dessert.

"I'm happy to get us started," he offered and she tried to focus on something other than his perfect mouth, his big, strong hands, the telltale bulge in his pants.

"Go ahead. I can't stop you." She'd be sorely disappointed now if they didn't see this game through to its inevitably sexy outcome.

"I wish you hadn't worn that outfit tonight."

"Why?"

"Covering up all that gorgeousness. It felt like you were punishing me."

She blushed again. That was exactly what she'd intended to do.

"But that was before I realized how hot it would be to unwrap you."

Julie clenched her thighs together as wet warmth seeped from her core. Her mouth had gone dry and her heart was racing.

"Your turn," Ty said.

She clamped her lips together. Shook her head. "I don't know how."

But he was persuasive. "The more I know about what makes you feel good, the better I can make you feel."

She practically had an orgasm right then and there.

"Tell me what you liked," he urged.

Everything. But she couldn't tell him that.

So then why were the words "I liked everything" bouncing around the limo?

He didn't smile now, just sat there with every muscle tensed.

For the first time, Julie realized she could be in control. If she forgot about being the perfect lady and gave in to her sexuality, she could turn this game around, pin Ty in a corner of desire.

"Tell me what I should have done differently," he said.

She inhaled deeply, taking in the musky scent of their lovemaking, the hint of cedar and spice that would always make her think of him.

"Nothing."

His voice was soft. "Then tell me what to do next."

She couldn't have formed words if there was a gun to her head.

"Tell me what you want me to do when we get back to your house, when we're all alone again. Just you and me."

He was doing it again, taking control of her mind, her entire body, and it was so hard for her to remember that she could have the same kind of power over him.

She shifted so that the hem of her dress rose up her thigh several inches. She played with the pearls at her neck to focus Ty's attention on her breasts and throw him off just as much as he'd thrown her.

"I want to take a bath."

A small muscle jumped in his jaw. Julie held back a victorious smile.

"Together."

He shifted uncomfortably, betraying his pent-up sexual energy.

Something wild and new bloomed into life within Julie's chest. For the first time ever, she had free reign to create and express her sexual fantasies. Nothing would shock Ty—yet she didn't feel like she needed to be kinky to impress him, either.

She could just be herself.

Ty obviously had faith in her unleashed sensuality, and if she did exactly what she wanted to really do, the next two weeks with Ty could be a little scary.

And incredibly exciting.

"Tell me more," he begged.

"Patience is a virtue," she teased. "Especially when it comes to pleasure."

He spread his legs, revealing his arousal. "I haven't wanted to play with myself this bad since I was a kid."

"Do you want me to stop?" she asked, hiding a smile.

"Hell no!"

"Good. Because before we bathe, you're going to take off your clothes while I watch. Don't forget to flex a little, show off for me."

"Will do," he murmured.

"Do you want to know what would *really* turn me on?"

"More than anything."

"I want you to get into the tub first. I want to know you're waiting for me, hard and ready, while I slowly undress."

He swallowed hard and she wanted to press a kiss to his Adam's apple, wanted to run her tongue over every inch of his body.

"And then what?"

She closed her eyes, laid her head back against the leather headrest. "And then I'm going to sink down on your cock and fuck your brains out."

She could hear his rapid breathing, which matched hers. Her pulse was jumping and she was this close to forgetting about his driver having a front-seat view to their sex show. The slightest touch from Ty and she was going to explode.

After what had to have been the longest wait of her life, they finally pulled up to her curb. She wasn't normally rude enough to shoot out of the car and run up her steps without thanking the driver, but she'd apologize to Jose later.

She'd just turned the key in her lock when Ty's hand snaked around hers and opened the door. Next thing she knew, they were inside her foyer and she was up against the wall with her dress pushed up to her waist.

"I really, really like your bathtub plan," he said, "but I'm afraid I'm not going to make it any farther than your front door."

A hot wave of arousal hit her and she ripped at his pants and shirt as he pulled another condom out of his jacket and ripped it open.

"Hurry," she said and a moment later he was shoving the crotch of her panties aside, and she was wrapping her legs around him again. He plunged his enormous erection all the way in, then out, then in again, harder, deeper this time, and she was crying out his name, begging him for more, sobbing as the orgasm she'd been waiting for shook her whole body. Again and again he rocked into her, until he stilled and she felt him pulsing inside her.

Yet again she gave thanks for his powerful physique, for the job that had perfectly trained him to hold her as if she weighed nothing at all.

His torn clothes lay on the floor, ripped apart by her greedy, lusty hands.

"I hope you packed more than one suit," she teased.

His soft chuckle reverberated through her rib cage.

At last, she understood why so many women pursued Ty, why they were willing to give up anything for one night—or more, if they were fortunate—with him. He knew how to make a woman feel good.

Not just how to give her pleasure, but also how to tap into her inner vixen and laugh with her at the same time.

Last week she never would have admitted that he was more than a playboy jock who could barely add or spell. But now she knew that Ty Calhoun was so much more complicated and wonderful than he ever let people know. Her stomach hurt when she thought about going their separate ways once her assignment had ended and his new season started.

Still, she had nearly two weeks with the most sexually fulfilling man on the planet, and she was going to squeeze every ounce of pleasure from them. As long as she didn't make the mistake of letting herself fall in love with him, she'd be just fine.

"Ready for that bath?" she asked, smiling as he carried her down the hall.

CHAPTER EIGHTEEN

Bright and early the next morning, Julie's Black-Berry buzzed a reminder that they had to be in Lake Tahoe by noon for another big fund-raiser. Ty would have been hard-pressed not to do her in the limo during the four-hour drive north if they hadn't both needed to catch up on sleep.

A couple of hours into the event, Julie found him sitting at a table signing autographs for a very long line of kids and their parents.

She handed him a bottled water and leaned over to whisper, "How's it going? Need a break anytime soon?"

He inhaled her cinnamon and cream scent and immediately got a boner. He wished he hadn't agreed to keep their relationship under wraps. He wanted to pull her onto his lap in front of everyone and kiss her. He wasn't sure if she realized that everyone pretty much thought she was his girlfriend, that a guy like him didn't have a gorgeous handler if he wasn't doing her.

Still, a promise was a promise. And he didn't want to do anything that could mess up the good thing they had going.

"I'm fine," he said, liking the way Julie looked with the Lake Tahoe pines behind her. He used to think a woman like her would only fit in at fancy cocktail parties or shopping at Tiffany's, but after watching her in action, he knew she had the stamina of an athlete and was willing to go the distance for her clients. "Were you able to block out the afternoon?"

She nodded. "As soon as you're done here, we're free until tonight's gala at Northstar Lake Tahoe."

Before turning back to his fans he added very softly, "Glad to hear it. I hope you're ready to get all wet."

Out of the corner of his eye, he watched her nipples harden through her dress. She really did have a dirty mind. Little did she know he was just talking about taking a dip in a private beach he knew about deep in the pines.

Her hip brushed against his shoulder as she walked away, branding him all over again with desire.

An hour later, he left his signing table and returned

to Julie's side to shake their host's hand. "It was great meeting so many Outlaws' fans. We'll see you tonight," he said, leaving no chance for anyone to waylay them.

"What took you so long?" she accused, nearly outpacing him in her urgency to get back to their rental convertible.

"Didn't you once tell me that patience was a virtue?"

She got into the passenger seat and glared at him. "You can't say something like that to me in front of everyone."

"Like what?" he asked, enjoying winding her up—and then helping her let off steam in the best way possible.

"'I hope you're ready to get wet,'" she mimicked.

He turned the key, started driving. "No one heard. Besides, I figured it would be nice to take a break for a few hours, hang out by some water."

Her face flamed as she realized she'd turned his comment into a sexual innuendo.

Still, she turned on him. "Could you have signed any slower? You really don't need to ask people about their dogs. Their kids are enough."

Fortunately, after a no-holds-barred night together, he didn't have to think twice before saying exactly what was on his mind.

"Looks like someone needs to come."

"No thanks to you," she muttered.

To hell with making her wait any longer. He might as well oblige right then and there.

He glanced over at her bare thighs on the leather passenger seat, then slid his right hand over to her lap.

"What are you doing?" she bit out, but her legs had already opened to him, just enough that he knew she wanted him to touch her, to get her off at least once on the way to their next wet and slippery destination.

"Tiding you over," he said as he slid the fabric up her thighs so that he could get at her slick, wet pussy.

"You're driving."

He grinned. "Don't worry, I've got it covered."

She wasn't arguing anymore so he got back to business.

"Open your legs for me, sweetheart. I want to feel how wet you are."

The wind carried away her small whimper, and when she relaxed her thighs, his cock nearly exploded in his jeans. His fingers found the edge of her panties and they were already damp.

"How long have you been waiting for me to touch you?" he asked, his voice silky, his cock throbbing.

"Hours. It felt like forever."

He tried to find his breath and it was damn hard. She was the girl of his dreams. Every guy's fantasy. A sex goddess.

She was smart, funny, and successful too, but it made Ty nervous having such strong feelings about anything other than sex.

Fortunately, pleasuring Julie was job one. He dipped one finger into her honey, relishing her slick heat as he slid his middle finger from one end of her plump lips to the other.

"Ty, please," she begged and he knew she wanted him to swirl her clit, to press down on it until she screamed.

First things first. He shifted his wrist so that he could slide one finger into her, then two, pumping them in and out in a slow, steady rhythm. He never got tired of touching her, never got tired of being inside her, with his fingers, his tongue, his cock.

She rocked her hips into his hand, holding his wrist hostage with her hands, and he knew she was close to coming, whether or not he ever gave her clit the attention it deserved.

"Let me see how horny you are," he urged, and she let go of his hand so that he could find her hard bead, letting him work it, rub against it.

Her whole body tensed beneath his hands, and he said, "I want to hear you come."

The road was deserted and she was as hot for him as she'd ever been. His name was on her lips, first a whisper and then a moan of deep, deep pleasure as he left her clitoris, slipped his fingers in her, moving back and forth between her clit and lips over and over again, as fast as he could.

Her legs fell all the way open, her head pressed into the headrest as she arched her back. Her nipples were hard against the fabric of her dress and he loved watching her as she came with wild abandon.

Wetness coated his fingers and he continued stroking her as her orgasm rocked all the way through her. Just in time, they made it to the small, private house on the lake that he'd borrowed from one of his old friends. He put his foot on the brake and reluctantly took his hand out from between her legs.

"Here we are. Hope you enjoyed the ride."

She opened her eyes and looked out at the incredibly blue pond. It was nearly a mile long and half a mile wide. He'd seen a lot of beautiful things in his life, but this particular combination of water and trees and mountains was darn near perfection.

All it needed to send it over the edge was the perfect woman.

His brain shut down for a long second.

Was Julie the perfect woman?

He got out of the car, then went to the trunk as if he needed something out of it. Any excuse to get a grip and figure out what the hell was wrong with him.

Sure, the sex had been amazing—perfect, even.

But that didn't mean jack, not when they hardly saw eye-to-eye when they had their clothes on. And especially not when they came from totally different worlds.

She would always belong to the rich and privileged.

He would always be the hero of the underdogs.

So sure, he'd continue to fuck her brains out for the next two weeks; only an idiot would turn that opportunity down. But he was going to keep everything else shut down—his heart, his emotions, whatever part of him was capable of loving. He'd be a fool not to.

He shut the trunk, then dropped the keys onto the front seat. Sitting down on a rock, he slipped off his shoes and balled his socks up inside them.

Julie's face was radiant with wonder. "This is beautiful, Ty. Absolutely incredible."

He nodded, took in the view again. "Only the best for you," he said, trying like hell to keep the edge off his words. He didn't want to sound like an ass and scare her away.

She gave him a sharp look and he knew he'd better smooth things over if he wanted the afternoon to go as well as the car ride had.

"Ever gone for a swim in Tahoe?"

She kicked off her heels and walked through the

sand to the water's edge. "No way. The water can't be more than seventy degrees in the middle of summer."

He pulled his Outlaws T-shirt over his head, then threw it onto his shoes and socks. Her gaze roved hungrily over his chest and he knew she was already heating back up.

"I'll keep you warm," he said, knowing it was a cheesy line, but also the truth.

She shook her head, backing away from the shore. "And don't think you can tempt me by taking off your pants."

He undid the top button on his jeans. "You do know you're going in, even if I have to carry you myself, don't you?"

Her nipples did that hardening thing again and he said, "Take your clothes off, already."

She laughed, still backing away from both him and the water's edge.

"Only you would ask a woman to strip in such a totally offhand way. *And* expect her to do it."

He was down to his boxers—and the perpetual hard-on he wore whenever Julie was within a hundred feet—by the time he started stalking toward his beautiful prey.

"You wouldn't dare," she said, gesturing to her dress.

"Wanna bet?"

He scooped her up in his arms and anticipation vibrated through her limbs.

"You're going to pay for this," she said, but there was no anger behind her words, only heat, and a desperation that matched his.

"I'm going to hold you to it," he murmured in her ear as he walked slowly into the cold water. "I've been waiting for you to dominate me all week."

He felt her thighs clench, watched her nipples rise up. Water lapped over his thighs and he bent his head down to her breasts, covering the thin fabric with his mouth, sucking and pulling at her nipples.

"I'll do anything you want," she gasped as she arched into his swirling tongue, "just please don't make me go in the water."

"Anything?"

She nodded, looked him in the eye. "Anything."

So many pictures rushed through his head in that moment, he nearly dropped her. Pulling her tightly against him, he took a breath.

And picked a fantasy.

"Deal."

He turned around and headed for a shady spot beneath an enormous pine. He laid her down on her back, her skirt riding up her thighs, showing him a sliver of panties. His cock throbbed.

She lay back on her elbows, watching him, waiting for his demands. He licked his lips.

"I want to watch you play with yourself."

Julie sat up. "What?"

She didn't refuse, though. Already, he knew she was thinking about touching herself while he watched. And it was making her crazy.

He lay down next to her on his side, propping his head on one hand. "I want to see you run your hands down your naked body. Over your breasts. Onto your pussy. I want to see your fingers slide over your lips, swirl your clit. I want to watch you make yourself come. I want you to know I'm watching. To know how much I want to be where your hands are."

Breathing fast, she stared at him. Then she turned her back to him, saying, "You'd better unzip me so I can get started."

And Ty suddenly wondered if he could survive this after all.

CHAPTER NINETEEN

Ty's fingertips brushed down her spine as he pulled her zipper down. He was a master of touch; even the slightest brush of his fingers made her wet and ready for him.

Her dress had a built-in shelf bra, so when she shimmied the pink cotton down her hips, all that remained were her soaked panties, a sensation she was getting used to after a week of constant arousal.

"Everything off," he growled. His shoulder muscles and biceps were taut, and his cock was thrusting out at her from beneath his cotton boxers.

"Of course," she said. "Otherwise how could you watch me dip my fingers into my pussy?"

She hadn't said the P word before, and liked how naughty it made her feel. Ty's eyes turned a dark, deep brown and his cock twitched as a spot of moisture appeared on his boxers.

Hooking her thumbs into the thin silk strand that held up her panties on both sides, she slowly slid them off her hip bones, over her mound, down her thighs.

"I feel so naughty lying here naked in the sand," she murmured softly, enjoying his answering groan as she lay back on her dress.

Arching her back slightly, she closed her eyes and moved her hands to the top of her chest, just below her chin. She could feel his eyes on her breasts, and her nipples ached with pleasure from the few moments he'd sucked them. God, she loved his mouth on her.

She slid her hands down the sides of her rib cage and cupped her breasts. Pretending her fingers were his lips, she reached for her nipples, tugged and pulled at them, barely hearing Ty's "Holy shit, you're hot" as she focused on the sensations working their way from her tits straight to her belly.

Leaving one hand on her breasts, she ran the other down her flat stomach. Opening her legs, she let them fall to the side, wanting to expose herself to both her hand and Ty's devouring eyes.

With her middle finger, she found the hard nub of her clitoris, and she was almost afraid to touch it, knowing how close she was to coming again. She didn't want to go too fast; didn't want either of them to miss out on the full show.

Still, she couldn't resist teasing herself, couldn't stop her finger from sliding over her clit and pressing into it. She gasped and made herself pull away.

"That's right," Ty coaxed, "nice and slow."

His warm voice rushed over her, taking aim at her nipples and her pussy. She wanted to slide her fingers inside herself, imagine he was touching her, knowing that he would be doing just that very, very soon, anywhere and any way she desired.

Raising her hips slightly, she tightened her stomach muscles and slid her hand back down over her mound.

"Am I doing it right?" she whispered, not stopping for his answer because it felt so good.

"Sweet Lord, yes," he groaned and she smiled through her arousal.

She spread her legs even wider and slid her middle finger in, first just the tip, and then up to her second knuckle. Knowing he was holding his breath, she pushed her finger in to the hilt. Moving her hips in rhythm with her hand, she rocked back and forth, sliding her finger all the way out then all the way back in. She was so close to coming, all it would take was half a second on her clit and she'd explode.

Unable to hold out another second, she slipped her finger out and finally touched her clit. Once the dam had broken, she couldn't stop circling, swirling the taut flesh. She wasn't in control of her hips and hands anymore; they were controlling her. Her other hand kneaded and rolled her nipples as she orgasmed in plain sight on a private beach in Lake Tahoe under a pine tree.

Her limbs were shaking uncontrollably as she opened her eyes. Ty's hand was on his cock and she nearly came all over again at the frantic way he was working it.

"Don't you dare waste that," she gasped, and a second later he had a condom on and was thrusting into her, one thumb on her clit, pushing her straight toward another amazing orgasm, the other hand on her breasts and his mouth on hers.

✳

Julie sat on the enormous porch overlooking the lake, sipping a glass of mineral water. After their incredible lovemaking, she and Ty had gone into the house to clean up and get dressed again. They had to leave for his evening engagement in a half hour and it was nice to get some quiet time together.

He appeared with a plate of fresh bruschetta and her stomach growled. "We really need to send your friend a thank-you letter." She put one in her mouth and closed her eyes in ecstasy. "Wow. These are great."

Ty said. "I think you've already met the owner. Dominic was working out at the gym with me. He spoke to you, made you laugh."

Julie cocked her head to the side, thought for a moment. "Hmm . . . I'm getting a picture of a really gorgeous man with black hair and green eyes."

Something that looked suspiciously like jealousy crossed Ty's face. "He's a great guy."

"He's not my type."

Ty visibly relaxed, and sat beside her on the soft outdoor couch.

"Good. Because I'd have to rip him apart with my bare hands if he ever touched you."

Julie didn't know what to say to his surprisingly touching declaration. It was nice to know that they had an unspoken agreement of monogamy for their time together. She certainly couldn't have dealt with him even looking at another woman. Not while they were sleeping together.

Although, if she was honest with herself, it was just as hard for her to think about Ty dating someone else when her contract with the Outlaws came to an end.

She looked back out over the water, let herself soak up the beauty, the small waves rippling across the lake onto the shore. Inhaling the sweet pine scent, she softly said, "I'm having a great time with you, Ty."

She didn't look at him; didn't want to see if he felt the same way, or if he was trying to hide pity at how quickly she'd fallen for him. But at the same time, she wanted him to know that she was happy. And that she was pleased with the work he'd done thus far to clean up his act.

"I'm glad," was his response.

There was so much warmth in the two words that her fears instantly disappeared. What was she thinking? They were evenly matched, both in spirit and accomplishment. There was nothing but lots more fantastic sex, along with laughter, in their near future.

CHAPTER TWENTY

The next day, they headed for a children's football camp in Palo Alto. "This is my favorite place to be all summer," Ty told Julie as they pulled into the Camp Cougar parking lot. Several football fields stretched all around the parking lot, with a brown-shingled building directly to their left. "Come on, I'll introduce you to the guys who run this place."

It was bear hugs all around inside camp head-quarters.

"Everyone, this is Julie." Ty wasn't embarrassed about needing an image consultant, but he wouldn't have minded letting his friends think they were an item for five minutes.

Julie, of course, didn't feel the same way. As she shook hands she said, "I own an image consultancy, and the Outlaws hired me to work with Ty."

"I hope we're not supposed to act surprised," Tony

said with a grin. Now in his sixties, he'd been running this camp since Ty was a ten-year-old on the field, kicking ass and taking names. "Ty always was a wild one—although we loved him anyway."

"What have we got this year?" Ty asked, not in the mood to discuss his past. Things were so good with Julie that he didn't want her remembering what an ass he'd been in high school. "Any standouts?"

Tony nodded. "One kid, Jack, reminds me a lot of you. He can play any position, offense, defense. Nothing fazes him. Plays like he's sixteen, not ten."

Julie sat down on the corner of a desk and crossed her legs. Damn, she had some sweet thighs, Ty thought.

"Does being so good, so young, ever lead to resentment from the other kids?"

Julie's question was a good one, and Ty struggled to focus on football rather than what was beneath her panties. "Sometimes there are problems, especially if one of the kids has an attitude. In most cases it isn't really their fault, though. It can be rough when your folks have been building you up to be the next Payton Manning."

Tony nodded. "This kid, Jack, is real friendly, just like your client here. Attracts people like a magnet."

Ty took the compliment in stride and looked out the open sliding glass door, scanning the field. It wasn't hard to spot the future superstar. He threw like a high school kid, not a fifth grader. He was quick and seemed to have an instinctive understanding of the game. While the other kids had to stop, think, then decide which way to turn, Jack was two steps ahead.

"You ready to meet this year's group? They've been talking about you since yesterday."

Ty nodded. "Can't wait."

＊

If someone had told Julie that she'd thoroughly respect Ty Calhoun, she would have said they were completely nuts. But somewhere along the way, she'd developed a newfound appreciation for Ty's charisma and charm, not only at the handful of charity functions they'd attended together throughout Northern California, but also from watching him interact with these kids.

She'd called a photographer and several sports writers to let them observe Ty working with the kids. By the time her assignment was through, people were going to remember him for the great things he did, not for cavorting with strippers.

Sitting in the shade of an oak tree, she sent one final email and dropped her BlackBerry back into her bag.

Ty was showing the kids how to hold and throw the ball, and they were eagerly taking in his every word, every movement. As a group, they picked up their footballs and tried to mimic the way he turned and cocked his arm, the perfect spiral the ball took through the air. For the most part, it was a ball-flinging disaster, and Julie quielty giggled. The boy they'd been talking about, Jack, was the only kid in the bunch who made it look easy.

In so many ways, he was a smaller version of Ty. Dark hair, tanned skin, effortless grace on the field. If she and Ty had a child, would it be a boy who looked like Jack? Or a little girl with blonde hair and blue eyes?

Her hand went to her mouth as she gasped. She hadn't actually just imagined having a child with Ty, had she?

She was letting herself get in *way* too deep. She took a deep breath, working hard to rebuild the wall around her heart. How could she have let herself forget, for one single moment, what he'd done ten years ago?

Julie's eyes blurred as she watched Ty run across the grass to pick up a football. All at once, she was back in that yacht with the eighteen-year-old boy she'd just given her soul to.

*

Grad night on Ty's borrowed yacht was an endless dream of pleasure. Hour after hour, Ty continued to kiss her, lick her, and caress her, and she returned the favor in every way she could. She wanted to memorize every muscle, every sinew, the way his abs tightened when she swept her tongue across his nipples and then marked them gently with her teeth.

Sated and overwhelmed by all of her orgasms, hardly able to believe how close she felt to a boy she'd never talked to before that night, Julie lay half-awake inside the stateroom until the light outside the tiny window changed from moonlit black to gold.

"It's morning," she whispered and Ty answered by pulling her closer against him, his eyes still closed. When she finally fell asleep, she dreamed that she was sailing across the Bay. The wind was in her hair and it was a perfect, sunny day. But then she saw Ty piloting an oncoming yacht that was just about to crash into her. She cried out for him to change course, but all he did was laugh at her. His friends were on board his ship and they were all laughing too, like they knew some dirty little secret about her.

Julie woke up just as the ships were about to hit. She was disoriented on so little sleep, but she was pretty sure she heard stomping on the deck above them. Had the owners come back early to claim their boat?

She sat up, covering herself with the sheet. But even though she was petrified about being discovered having sex on a stranger's boat, she couldn't help but admire Ty's incredible physique, tanned and toned from the ankles up.

His eyes opened and his lips curved in a sexy grin. "Come lie down again," he drawled, but she couldn't ignore the feet that got louder with every passing second.

"It sounds like someone's on board," she whispered.

He cocked his head at the ceiling. "Sure does."

She knew her eyes had to be wild, her hair and makeup unfixable. "Shouldn't we get dressed and get out of here?"

He sat up, utterly unconcerned with his nakedness. Julie didn't think she'd ever learn to be so comfortable with her body, not if she had a hundred years to practice.

"I'm not too worried about it," he said, "but I can go out and take a look if you really want me to."

She nodded. "That'd be great."

While he was gone, she'd put her dress back on and use the tiny bathroom to assess the rest of the damage. After all, she was going to have to sneak back into her parents' house soon. Although they were both so self-absorbed, she doubted they'd notice that she'd been out all night and hadn't called.

He zipped up his black dress slacks, picking up her discarded panties and shoving them in his pocket.

"Just to make sure you don't try and leave before I get back."

Almost at the door, he turned, came back to her, and kissed her hard. "Thanks for a great night," he said, grinning as he let her go and opened the door.

Julie blankly watched the door close behind him. How had he meant that? Were you supposed to thank your lover after a night of great sex? Or was he trying to tell her they were done now?

She took a deep breath. When he came back down she'd talk to him so that she'd know if they were officially dating now. He was going to USC on a football scholarship, but his school was only an eight-hour drive from Stanford, so they could see each other several times a month pretty easily if they really wanted to.

She was working on the zipper on her badly wrinkled dress when she heard laugher. Her spine tingled with alarm. Who was Ty laughing with? And what was he laughing about?

He couldn't be laughing about her, could he? Not after what they'd shared. She'd given him her virginity. He had to know how special he was to her—that she wasn't like the girls he usually slept with.

She finger-combed her hair and quickly looked in the mirror over the tiny sink to make sure she didn't have mascara on her face. She told herself that she trusted him to tell her the truth when he came back down. Even so, she picked up her heels and tiptoed down the hall and partway up the stairs, just to the point where she could see some faces and hear what they were saying.

One of Ty's teammates poured something golden into a shot glass and handed it to Ty. "Dude, you need to tell us who you're here with. Everyone's been wondering."

Ty tilted his head back and drank, then held out the small glass for a refill. "Trust me, she's hot."

Julie's face flamed and she nearly dropped her shoes. How could he talk about her like she was just some random girl he'd picked up at a party? Even if, a voice inside her admitted, that was exactly what she was.

"Samantha? Ellen? Melissa?"

Ty laughed and did another shot. "I'll see you guys later. Got to get back to the fine babe I've got stashed away."

Julie hated the way he called her a "fine babe," even though she knew lots of girls would be flattered.

"What's that in your pocket?" one of his friends said, grabbing her underwear. "Hell yeah, you've got another pair of panties for your collection!"

En masse, Ty's friends dropped to their knees. "We bow down to the master."

Ty made no move to get her underwear back. Instead, he inclined his head to his friends as if he was the king and they were his servants.

He'd taken her panties to give to his friends as a prize.

Cold, bitter anger filled Julie. She walked back down the stairs and pushed open the stateroom door. Eyeing the rumpled bed with distaste, she sat down on a firm upholstered chair in the corner by the built-in armoire.

A few minutes later Ty returned, his eyes glazed over enough to make her wonder how many more shots he'd pounded.

"Miss me?" he asked, but his expression made it perfectly clear that she had to know how lucky she was to be his chosen grad night screw.

"Not really," she forced herself to say in a steady voice. "I'd like my underwear back now."

He shook his head and moved toward her. "Not so fast. We've got hours before the owner comes back. Don't you want to make the most of it?"

Self-disgust washed through her. Had she really let him touch her all over? Go inside her? He was just a cocky jerk looking to score.

"I don't want to keep you from your friends. I'll bet they missed you last night."

He shrugged. "Not really."

"Funny, that's not what it sounded like from here."

He kneeled in front of her on the expensive carpet, at least acting like he cared. Considering how drunk he probably was, he moved pretty fast. She'd heard his dad was a drunk too. Like father, like son.

"Forget what you heard," he said. "It's just stupid guy stuff."

"Screw you."

He grabbed her hand. All night long, his touch had inflamed her, driven her crazy with desire. Now her fingers remained as cold as icicles.

"It was just guy talk. They wouldn't understand about you."

She didn't give a crap about his pseudo apologies. She couldn't let herself believe him.

Julie pulled her hand out of his warm grasp, then stood and stepped into her shoes as if she didn't give a damn that he was on his knees staring at her.

He stood up too, and she hated how dwarfed she felt by his height, his broad shoulders, as if he was lording his size over her on purpose.

"I said I was sorry, but you're not going to listen to what I have to say, are you?"

She stared straight back at him. "I hate you. I'll always hate you. And I never, ever want to see you again."

He reached for his shirt and grabbed his shoes. "Fine by me. Have a nice life."

He left her standing in the middle of the boat. She hadn't even been able to get away first. It was the final blow.

✳

Julie's eyes refocused on the football field as Ty laughed and picked up one of the smaller kids. He spun the little boy around to celebrate what she guessed was a perfect spiral.

How could she go back to putting up walls when he acted like that?

✳

It had been a great day. Ty was clear on what he wanted to do when the time came to retire. He wanted to run a place like this, teach kids the joy of the game, how everything you needed to know about life was right there with you on the field. Teamwork, respect, how to win, and how to lose.

Football was hard on a body. Either you were forced to retire injured or you left willingly while everything still worked. Ty was hoping for the latter.

As he helped the boys clean up the balls and nets on the fields, he looked over at Julie. She had her head bent over her BlackBerry, good little worker that she was. He was hit with the memory of taking her naked up on that balcony in Napa and he had to look away, trying to get his mind off of her curves, the way the pulse in her neck jumped when she threw her head back and came. He was about to turn around and head for the clubhouse when he heard a man's rough voice boom across the field.

"Jackie boy, I hope you kicked some ass today."

Jack's face flamed and he ducked his head and fumbled a ball on purpose so that he could run after it. Away from the man that Ty assumed was his father.

The ruddy-faced man stumbled in Ty's direction. He slapped Ty on the back and stale whisky fumes poured out of his mouth as he said, "That's some superstar I've got out there, isn't it, Ace?"

Ty worked to repress his revulsion. It wasn't Jack's fault that his father was a worthless drunk.

"Sure is. He's a great kid."

The man scowled. "All I care about is that he's great at football. We didn't come here this week for him to make friends. Win at all costs—that's what I've been teaching him. I don't care who he has to crush along the way. He hasn't been a sniveling baby out here today, has he?"

Ty had gone cow tipping a few times with his buddies as a kid in Marin, and he was sorely tempted to poke this guy's overinflated chest and watch him fall to the ground, his thick legs flailing heedlessly in the air.

But he wasn't here to tell guys like this where to stick it. All he could do was help their kids on the field, teach them the right way to act, and hope they remembered what he'd told them when push came to shove.

Ty said, "He's doing great," and headed across the field toward Jack. He squatted down and covered Jack with his back, making sure his father couldn't see either of their faces.

"I met your dad."

The kid's eyes shuttered, so different from how open and receptive he'd been all day. "It's no big deal. I can handle him."

Ty nodded. "Sure you can." He paused. "He

reminds me a lot of my dad. Says the same kind of stuff."

Jack looked up in surprise. "You're kidding, right?"

"My dad put a lot of pressure on me too. Winning was the only thing he cared about."

Jack screwed up his face. "But isn't winning what matters most?"

Ty reached into his pocket, pulled out paper and a pen, and wrote his cell number on it. "Sometimes it does. Other times you just go out there and play the best game you can." He handed the scrap of paper to Jack. "You need anything, you give me a call."

Jack looked down at Ty's cell number, his mouth open. "Wow."

"Even if you just need to talk, call me. If I can't pick up right away, I promise to call you back."

They both heard Jack's father coming and the boy shoved the paper into his pocket before his dad could see. Ty knew damn well how his own father would have reacted to having the personal telephone number of a pro player way back when. He would have gone straight to the bar to buy everyone a round to celebrate. Before the night was through, that number would have been passed into every stranger's hand.

Ty watched Jack and his father walk away, wondering if he'd just made a mistake, when Julie appeared at his side.

"You look serious," she said, following his gaze to the parking lot.

He shook off his dark mood. One thing he had no intention of ever discussing with Julie was his father. She knew he'd been a drunk—shit, everyone in town knew, and once he'd gone pro the press had told the world—but it still wasn't something he talked about much. Over the years, the more games he'd won, the more people left his past alone. And that was exactly how he liked it.

"You're looking at a future superstar," he said, changing the subject.

"I know next to nothing about football, and even I can see Jack is talented." She frowned. "But his father seemed a little intense, didn't he?"

More like drunk off his ass, Ty thought.

Julie took a deep breath, seemed like she wanted to say something to him. He was learning her body signals. She was holding something back.

"Spit it out."

She laughed. "I never knew how transparent I was."

"Only to me," he said and their eyes locked for a long moment. "You sure I can't kiss you right now?"

Her mouth opened slightly and he almost did it anyway. Finally, she shook her head. "You can't."

He scowled. "Explain to me again why you're so intent on keeping our relationship a secret?"

"You can't seriously need me to explain the boundaries of a client relationship, can you?"

"Do you always treat your clients this well?"

Her hands balled at her sides and she lowered her voice. "Why are you acting like this?"

He realized he was being an ass because—God, it felt stupid to even think the words—his feelings were hurt. She didn't want anyone to know she was sleeping with a dumb jock. So what? She wasn't any good for his image, either. Sure, she was beautiful. But people expected him to date fun girls. Not women who owned their own businesses and knew which fork to use.

"It's been a long day out here with these kids," he lied. "Forgive me?"

She stared at him and he waited impatiently for her to make up her mind. He'd go nuts if she decided he'd pushed her too far.

Finally, she nodded. "You're forgiven," she said, "but I have to admit I have ulterior motives."

He raised an eyebrow, immediately hoping her motives involved being naked and sweaty.

"Which are?"

"My parents called. They're having a big dinner party tomorrow night." She paused, looked guilty. "You're the guest of honor."

"Sounds like more of a command than an invitation."

She bit her lip. "I'm so sorry. My mother made it perfectly clear that she'll never forgive me if you don't show up and they end up with egg on their face. I feel really horrible about this, Ty." Big blue eyes turned to him. "You don't have to go. It's not your job to make my parents happy. I'll find some way to deal with them."

He touched her face, lightly running the side of his palm down her smooth cheek. He knew more than his share about how hard it was to deal with parents and their expectations. The least he could do was make this easy on her. She'd been great all week. It was time to take one for the team.

"I'm happy to go, Julie."

She turned her face into his palm. "Thank you."

Her lips brushed against his hand and blood rushed to his head. To both of them.

Tony called out from the deck off the clubhouse, "BBQ's on at my house."

Ty reluctantly dropped his hand. There were about a hundred things he'd rather do right now than eat hot dogs at his old friend's house. He'd be able to hang out with his friends forever. But where Julie was concerned, the clock was rapidly ticking down.

CHAPTER TWENTY-ONE

J ulie could hardly believe what a fantastic time she was having. Once, she would have automatically assumed that Ty's friends would be conceited jerks. They were all jocks or ex-jocks, after all. Instead she found them to be some of the nicest men she'd ever met. Warm, easygoing, confident.

But definitely not arrogant. There wasn't a chip in sight, even though they were very good at what they did and they'd earned a great deal of money.

She chatted with the football wives as the guys loudly cleaned up. It suddenly occurred to her that most of the guys she'd dated for the past decade—men in suits, entrepreneurs, fast-tracked vice presidents —were far more arrogant than any of these men who earned their living with their bodies.

After more football talk than she'd ever thought to hear in her life, she was just starting to grasp how much strategy and brainpower there was to the game.

Her parents had never encouraged her to play sports, and while she certainly put in her time on the elliptical trainer at the gym, working out was just a way to keep her figure intact.

Ty pushed his body with intense concentration and focus. Whether he was lifting weights, riding a stationary bike, or swimming laps, he didn't waste one second complaining or taking it easy. Being in peak physical condition was his job, and he took his responsibilities seriously.

Lucky her.

Tony's wife went to get her another nonalcoholic beer and Julie stared into the fire pit, amazed at how quickly her life had done a complete about-face. She was sitting outside by a fire wearing an oversized Outlaws sweatshirt to ward off the slight chill, getting hot and tingly thinking about a football star's big muscles.

"Let me guess what you're thinking about," Ty whispered into her ear and her nipples immediately went hard.

"You like kids, don't you?"

He sat down next to her and took a swig from his Coke. "Not exactly what I was hoping you'd say."

She grinned, lowered her voice. "Women think men who are great with kids are sexy."

He grinned back. "Now that's more like it."

Tony's grandkids were chasing each other around the lawn with water guns, screaming and laughing. "Ty, come save me," the littlest girl pleaded and he put down his soda and jogged over.

Even five-year-olds fell for Ty. He was utterly irresistible to every member of the female sex. And while he was all hers, she was going to enjoy every last bit of pleasure he offered.

＊

"Want to see one of the most beautiful things in the world?" Ty asked as they left Tony's front porch.

"I'd love to," she said.

Ty reached for her hand and led her down Tony's long, redwood-lined driveway. On the way to the barbecue, she realized that Tony had built his house on property adjoining the camp.

"Lucky bastard, getting to live down the road from a football field."

Julie pressed her lips together. She wasn't going to offer an unsolicited opinion. Everything was going so well between them, and it wasn't her place to tell him how to live his life. He had a fantastic mansion in one of San Francisco's most exclusive neighborhoods. He was already happy.

Without her.

Ty turned his head and looked at her, his features lit by the moonlight.

"You want to say something, you should say it."

"Your house is beautiful," she began and he held up a hand.

"Stop right there. You don't need to massage my ego. Hell, you're one of the few people who hasn't told me exactly what I want to hear in years. If you've got an opinion, I'd like to hear it."

Julie licked her lips, gripping his hand tighter. She took a deep breath. She never spoke out of turn, never said anything a client didn't want to hear, not unless she reworked it until it was totally palatable.

"Have you ever thought about moving? I mean, if you want to be somewhere more like this?"

He was quiet for a long moment, and her heart beat double-time. Less than a week ago she'd gone out of her way to publicly insult him. But now, she didn't want to hurt his feelings.

"When I was a kid, I used to dream about the house I was going to have. I'd ride over the Golden Gate Bridge and tool around Seacliff on my shitty bike, ranking the houses in order of which ones I'd buy."

She smiled. "I'm really impressed. You got what you wanted."

"The first year I lived there was all one big party. It's a great house."

"Amazing," she echoed.

"But I'm thinking it might be time for some changes."

She turned to look at him, surprised that he agreed with her. And what did he mean by *changes* with an *s*? Was she one of those changes?

They were standing on the edge of a football field she hadn't yet seen with stadium lights and bleachers. Ty walked over to a metal lockbox and flipped several switches. The grass turned bright green beneath the powerful lights.

Julie felt like they were standing in a private wonderland.

"See what I mean?" Ty said and she shot a glance at him.

He was facing the empty field with a look on his face that spoke volumes. Usually, he kept his true emotions well hidden behind teasing, and joking. Only during their lovemaking had she caught glimpses of another Ty. He always had such an easiness about him, but now in addition to his usual relaxed, confident stance, she saw joy too.

"I never thought I'd say this about a football field," she said, "but it is pretty amazing."

"Come out here," he said, pulling her forward.

"I've only seen one football game before in my whole life," she admitted. "On TV. This January. When you won the Super Bowl."

Surprise registered on his features, along with a healthy dose of delight. Julie was pleased that she could make him happy by divulging that she'd seen his amazing moves.

"Seriously? That's the only one?"

She laughed at his incredulous expression, "Believe it or not, some people just don't watch football."

He raised an eyebrow. "You never went in college with friends?"

She'd always made an excuse not to go, not wanting to be reminded of Ty in any way. "Not even the tailgates."

He shook his head. "I'm surprised you even know the word for pregame parties in parking lots."

Frustration welled up inside her. Didn't he know why she'd brought this whole subject up? Didn't he know how hard it was for her to risk thinking beyond the end of her assignment?

"What I'm trying to say is that I'd like to see a game," she spat out. "In a stadium. I'd like to see your talent in action."

"It's just what I do," he said, downplaying his natural ability yet again. He was given countless opportunities to toot his own horn as fans fawned all over him, yet he remained incredibly modest.

They moved down the field toward the stands and climbed halfway up before sitting down. Julie's skirt fluttered around her knees in the light evening breeze.

"Did you ever doubt yourself?" she asked, figuring they both knew she was talking about the final seconds of the Super Bowl.

His long, dark eyelashes rose and she lost her breath looking into his beautiful dark eyes.

"You want something bad enough, I figure you should go get it."

When he put it like that, everything sounded so simple. No doubts. No fears. Just pinpointing exactly what you wanted and going after it, knowing it could —and would—be yours.

All day, desire had been building within her, along with a longing to seize her remaining time with Ty, to make all of her fantasies come true before they said good-bye.

So far he'd been in the driver's seat, deciding when and where they'd had sex, instigating it each time. She hadn't let herself be in a position to be turned down, to be hurt by him.

"You want something bad enough, I figure you should go get it."

Ignoring how fast her heart was pounding, she said, "I had a really great time tonight. Only one thing could make it better."

Fire jumped in his eyes and she could have sworn he got an instant erection.

"What's that?" he asked, leaning back against the wood bleacher.

"I keep seeing this picture," she began slowly, "of you. Blindfolded." She stopped to let her words sink in.

"Go on."

"Naked."

He swallowed hard. Nodded. "Anything else?"

She shifted her hips on the hard bench, her skin already feeling tight and warm from the naughty little picture she was putting together.

"I believe you were tied up to something."

"We could have left right after dessert, you know."

His words were mild, but the desperation behind them belied his calm tone.

She licked her lips. "I'm not good at being rude."

"As long as you keep coming up with brilliant plans like this, you can be as polite as you want."

He pulled her into his arms and she felt so safe cushioned by his strength. He tipped her chin up so that she was looking at him.

"All day long, I want you," he said. "Every hour, I'm thinking about you. Touching you. Being with you."

"It's the same for me. Exactly the same."

He kissed her, his mouth caressing, tasting, telling her how much he wanted her. She moved closer, pressing her breasts into the hard wall of his chest, threading her fingers into his soft hair. She slipped her tongue into his mouth just as his hands covered her breasts, cupping and squeezing them until she was crying out into his mouth.

She moved her hands down his neck, over his shoulders, down his rippling pecs and abs until she found the hem of his Outlaws T-shirt. She lightly ran her fingers beneath the soft cotton. His stomach tightened and his lips hardened against hers. She felt herself sliding into that out-of-control place he always took her, and tried desperately to remember her original plan.

She wanted to show him what it was like to be at her mercy, slave to her every whim. And at the same time, she wanted to give him great pleasure, to show him in the most intimate way how special he was.

Pulling her mouth away from his, she asked, "Are you ready to make my vision a reality?"

He answered by pulling his T-shirt over his head. "Here's your blindfold."

She laughed in spite of the voice in her head that said he was too good at this, had obviously played this game many times with other women.

"Maybe we should head back to my house," she said, fighting the voice inside her that wondered why she'd decided to tell Ty about her secret fantasy.

Wasn't she just going to get burned even worse in the end?

She looked up and realized he was watching her closely.

"No one's going to disturb us," he said. "Especially not if the lights are out."

He walked down the bleachers, crossed the field, and flicked the lights off so that the field was bathed in the dim light of the moon.

Sex with Ty was risky and exciting, but it was more than just the crazy places they'd done it. No matter where they were, they shared an intense connection.

A connection she might never find with anyone else.

He gestured for her to join him at the base of the bleachers.

"There's one more way to make sure we don't give a free show to the neighbors."

Julie carefully negotiated the steep rows. With every step, she regained her sensual confidence. And when he pointed to the dark space beneath the stands, she could hardly wait to get down to the business of tying up her gorgeous temporary lover.

"Turn around," she said, in a sexy, take-no-prisoners voice, then tied his T-shirt around his eyes. While he had his back to her, she ran her hands over his incredible chest. His muscles tightened and flexed beneath her palms, and she pressed her breasts into his back, laying her cheek between his shoulder blades.

He smelled like freshly cut grass, and heat, and she let the memory imprint itself deep into her sub-conscious.

Slowly circling him, enjoying the view from every angle, she was pleased to see his erection straining hard against the zipper of his jeans. Giving thanks that her wraparound dress had a long belt, she quickly untied it and snapped it between her hands.

"Hands together above your head," she com-manded, going all the way up on her toes to tie the silk sash around his wrists. When she was finished she took a step back, loving how good he looked stretched out before her, waiting for her to touch him.

She tapped her finger on her lips. "I would tell you what I'm going to do next," she said, "but that would negate the point of the blindfold, wouldn't it?"

"I'm game for anything," he said, and she smiled.

So was she.

She undid the button of his jeans, letting her fin-gers slide over his cotton-covered cock as she pulled the zipper down.

Once she'd pushed his jeans down past his hips,

she slipped her finger into the slit of his boxers and found his silky smooth skin. She moved her finger up, then down the long, hard length. He groaned and wet heat flooded her. He didn't even have to touch her and she was on the verge of coming.

Part of her wanted to toy with him, to make him beg, but more than that, she wanted to take him in her mouth, feel him thrusting into her lips, her cheeks, her throat.

In a flash, she pulled down his boxers and was kneeling before him. His cock was beautiful and so perfect, standing proudly before her. She blew out a hot breath and a drop of pre-come emerged. She flicked out her tongue to taste him and he groaned again.

Grasping the base of his shaft with her hand, she licked her lips and moved his swollen head around the warm wetness of her mouth. She tasted his salty-sweet arousal and the next thing she knew she was sucking his thick member all the way into her mouth, down her throat, pulling at it with her cheeks while she pumped her hand on his shaft. Her other hand ran up his chest, and as he grew bigger and harder with every lash of her tongue, she groaned around his cock, urging him to let go.

He went completely still for a long moment before rocking feverishly against her lips. The next thing she knew, he'd worked loose from his silk binding and she was on her back on the soft dirt beneath the bleachers. He was lying above her, pushing her dress to the side, pulling her panties away from her wet pussy lips.

And then he was pushing into her and they were kissing and she felt so safe, so wonderfully safe with him that her climax came quickly and beautifully, the moon shining through the wooden stands, illuminating them both just enough that she could see him watch her as she came, with an expression that almost looked like love.

CHAPTER TWENTY-TWO

Ty's first thought when they arrived at Julie's parents' house the following evening was *Mine is bigger.* He almost laughed out loud at the ridiculous thought. Yet hadn't he spent years trying to outdo everyone around him? Everyone who had thought they were superior to the kid from the trailer park?

He'd done better than all of them combined. So much better, in fact, that it didn't seem to matter much anymore.

Julie climbed out of the backseat of the Rolls-Royce her parents had sent over, her movements uncharacteristically stiff. She looked like someone had shoved a poker all the way up her ass to her neck, and Ty couldn't help wondering if she was ashamed of being seen with him in front of her "people."

The previous night out on the football field, before she'd tied him up and had her way with him, had been the most they'd ever really talked. With any other woman, that would have been enough for Ty. Surprisingly, he'd started to hope for more.

"We don't have to stay long," she said, her voice clipped and strained. "Drinks and dinner, then we'll leave."

He adopted a relaxed stance, hoping it would rub off on her. "No worries. I'm happy to do whatever you need me to do."

She looked angry. "I don't need you to do anything. You shouldn't even be here." Forcefully clearing the mutinous expression from her face, she reached for his hand. "Thank you for doing this. You should be taking the night off, not be forced to schmooze with my parents' friends."

Ty wanted to pull her close to let her know that he'd play defense for her tonight, but his fingers had barely brushed over hers when she abruptly pulled hers away.

"Daddy!" she said in an abnormally high-pitched voice.

Ty looked up the winding, paved staircase to see if her father had changed much in ten years.

Nope. He was still lean, still tanned, still immaculately dressed. A Rolex watch gleamed on his wrist.

Ty's expression betrayed none of his dislike.

"You're late," was all Julie's father said in greeting.

She'd barely made an excuse about traffic when her father cut her off.

"Wonderful to see you again," he said to Ty.

Ty hadn't forgotten the day they'd met. He'd been a junior in high school and Julie's father had, like everyone else, wanted a piece of the superstar action. Ty was destined for the pros and lots of money. But first, he'd have to choose his launchpad.

Blake Spencer was a Notre Dame man, and he'd been sent to bring Ty on board using any means possible. Most sixteen-year-olds would have been awed by dinner at the Ritz—where the waiters hadn't asked for his ID—by the $1,000 bottle of champagne, the caviar, the filet mignon, and the hookers waiting in the limo after dinner.

But Ty was more comfortable getting burgers and talking strategy than he was with white tablecloths and waiters who bowed and scraped. He'd rather be out shooting pool with his friends than listening to some asshole go on and on about what great investments he'd made and how he ran his company with an iron fist. The couple of things Julie's dad said about football sounded weird, like he'd read them from a how-to book, or memorized a TV commentator's remarks.

So yeah, he remembered her dad. Only now did Ty stop to wonder why he'd never given Julie credit for surviving such a jerk of a father.

An invisible punch smashed into his solar plexus as the answer snaked through him: *Because you thought* you *were surviving the worst. No one else had it as bad as you, did they?*

"We were all thrilled when we found out our Julie was working with you."

Ty nearly cracked a smile. Julie sure as hell hadn't been pleased. Which had been a large part of her charm.

Her father continued braying into the silence. "A client like you is really going to raise her profile. She should be very thankful that the Outlaws thought of her."

Julie remained silent. Ty had gotten used to her quick comebacks, her smart mouth. He didn't like seeing her behave like this, reduced to nothing but a rich man's pretty daughter.

Exactly what he'd assumed she was back in high school.

Ty smiled thinly. "I insisted on working with her. I told my agent I wouldn't consider anyone else."

Gratitude practically seeped from Julie's pores. Ty wanted to smash her father's face in.

Her father blinked, then tried to usher Ty inside, leaving Julie standing alone by the limo. Ty tried to catch her eye but she was staring down at her shoes.

This was bullshit.

Ty pulled out of her father's grasp and returned to Julie. He tipped his finger under her chin, blocking her father's prying gaze with his broad back.

"We're a team," he said. "You've backed me up all week. Tonight you depend on me. Okay?"

Her eyes were bright and he held them for several beats until they refocused.

She spoke so softly, he could barely hear her. "Okay."

Ty kept his arm firmly tucked around Julie's waist as they walked through her front door. A young, stacked blonde smiled up at them.

"Oh goodie," she said, "you're here! I'm Susie and it's so exciting to meet you."

Ty knew thousands of women like this one and he'd slept with a fair number of them. Funny how one week with Julie had changed things—because he sure wasn't feeling it for this girl.

Sure, she was cute and had big tits. But he had a thing for interesting, smart women with great breasts. Julie fit the bill perfectly.

Julie stiffened against his arm. "I take it you're my father's new secretary."

The girl nodded happily. "Since April."

Ah, he got it. Blake was doing his secretary. And if he wasn't mistaken, he did girls like her on a regular basis.

Ty'd heard enough shrinks talk to the team to

know that when the people you trusted most cheated and lied, you learned not to trust anymore. Which went a long way to explaining Julie's initial aloofness to him. Sure, he'd screwed up in high school with her, but the way she'd held herself back from him went further than that.

Looking at her father and his newest "assistant" definitely clarified things.

Susie turned back to Julie. "Janie, you must feel so lucky to get to work with the legendary Ty Calhoun."

Julie's flinch was imperceptible to everyone except him, and he wished to hell they were anywhere but here. If only she'd told him that her father sucked balls, they could have blown off the party and had a good time somewhere, just the two of them.

"*Julie's* amazing," he said, emphasizing her name to Blake's little bimbo. "And I'm the lucky one."

He looked up and saw a faded, older version of Julie teetering down the wide, curving staircase. Everyone followed Ty's gaze, watching the woman grasp the rail tightly with each step. Her hair fell around her face like Julie's, and the shape of her mouth was similar as well.

She made it to the bottom of the stairs without once looking up. A waiter appeared with a tray of champagne and she reached for one, downing it quickly before exchanging it for a full glass and weaving her way into the living room.

All at once it hit him: Julie's mom was an alcoholic.

＊

Julie could feel herself shriveling up into a tight wad of shame. All she'd wanted was for her parents to act normal tonight in front of Ty.

Which, she supposed, was exactly what they were doing.

Her father had another new girlfriend posing as his assistant, and her mother was masking her shame with booze.

Julie hadn't wanted Ty to see this side of her. She felt raw, exposed, and sick to her stomach.

"Excuse me," she said, fleeing for the kitchen, which would be full of caterers who wouldn't pay any attention to her. Ty was going to have to float tonight on his own. She couldn't handle it.

She could only think of one place to find refuge, the place she'd always gone and hid as a child. Her bedroom. She took the back stairs two at a time and the years fell away.

She was three all over again, running away from her parents' fighting, scared of their loud voices, their ugly faces.

She was six, wondering why her mother was talking funny, messing up her words at the dinner table.

She was ten, hating her father for making her mother so sad by coming home late and missing dinner again, and hating her mother for being so weak and just taking it.

She was fourteen, running up the stairs to dream about the new boy at school, a football player who didn't even notice she was alive.

She was eighteen, coming home the morning after the most wonderful—and horrible—night of her life, where she lost her virginity to the school's superstar football player, the same boy who hadn't looked or spoken to her for four years.

And now she was nearly thirty, still running up these stairs, still hiding from everything she didn't want to face, still looking for someone to love who would love her back.

She turned right at the top of the stairs and for a split second she wondered what she was going to find behind her closed childhood bedroom door.

Holding her breath, she turned the gold knob. Everything was just as she'd left it. The Ralph Lauren floral bedspread, the *Phantom of the Opera* and *Les Mis* posters.

All the things she'd left behind were still here, gathering dust, waiting for her to return to them.

Her mother hadn't touched the room, hadn't put anything away. That would have been too big a project for Carol.

Suddenly, Julie wondered if they were more alike than she'd previously thought. After all, she hadn't been any more willing than her mother to deal with the memories and emotions that lingered in this room.

Maybe coming upstairs hadn't been a good idea, after all. Maybe she could sneak back downstairs and wait out the party in the limo. Her parents wouldn't notice her absence, not with her father focused on how impressed his guests would be by Ty and her mother drinking herself into oblivion.

A knock sounded on the door, then Ty's gorgeous frame filled the doorway.

"Mind if I join you?"

A mixture of relief and humiliation flooded through her. She was glad that she didn't have to pretend to be the happy daughter of the mansion with Ty; he'd see through that in a heartbeat. But now he knew her secrets.

He knew where she came from.

He knew what she'd been hiding.

"Sure," she said in a shaky voice. "Come in."

He stepped inside and the room shrank before her eyes. His broad shoulders and tall frame filled her bedroom, changed it in an instant from an innocent childhood hideout into something mysterious.

Dangerous.

"So this is where you grew up?" He looked at the bed. "Where you slept."

She swallowed, nodded.

"I've got to know—what did you wear to bed?"

Her cheeks flamed. "Not much," she admitted and he moved closer.

"Nice. Very nice." And then, "Good thing I didn't know that in high school. I already had a boner every time I saw you walk down the hall. Thinking about you naked in this bed would have pushed me over the edge."

Suddenly Julie wasn't thinking about her parents anymore, about how embarrassed she was at their behavior.

Instead all she could focus on was how good she felt whenever Ty was around. How much she wanted him.

"I have an idea," he said, sitting down on the edge of her single bed. A bed that had never seen a boy, and only the barest bit of masturbation.

"I'm all ears," she said, even though the more honest response was that she was all hormones, all the time, whenever he was around.

"Come here," he said, patting his lap.

She perched on the edge of his knee and he pulled her into him. His heat and his hard muscles branded her, took her breath away.

"Everyone is busy drinking and talking downstairs. I figure we've got a good hour to kill before dinner. Seeing your bed gave me some good ideas."

"I don't know if we should," she whispered.

"I do," he said with a wink, and in that moment, Julie couldn't stop herself from falling a little bit in love with Ty all over again.

CHAPTER TWENTY-THREE

Ty's hands were warm around her bottom. She lowered her mouth to kiss him and he was so tender, so careful with her. Finding out that her father was a cheat and her mother was a drunk could have been the perfect grenade to wave in front of her face. He could have used her shame to force her to back off, to cut him some breathing room during the next week.

Instead, he chose this tenuous moment to be kind to her. To "back her up."

She nipped at his lips, wondering why she'd ever thought that jocks were nothing but empty, muscle-bound shells. Because while Ty certainly had looks and charm to spare, he also had more than his share of warmth and understanding.

Pulling her lips away from his mesmerizing kiss, she said, "I'm ready to hear your ideas now."

She felt his erection stiffen even further against the back of her thigh.

He picked up one of her hands, traced the tops of each of her fingers with his thumb, then turned over her hand and pressed a kiss into her palm.

"I don't think I've thanked you yet for what you did to me last night under the bleachers."

Arousal sizzled deep in the base of her stomach. "You don't need to thank me," she said, her words breathless and excited. Something wonderful was on its way.

"I insist on returning the favor."

The lack of blood to her brain made her slow to pick up his implication.

"Oh," she finally said. "You want to . . ."

"Tie you up."

The sensual image hit her square in the chest and she gasped.

"Blindfold you."

She licked her lips, wondering how it was possible for her heart to beat so fast.

"Taste you."

She couldn't take her eyes from his, couldn't think of anything but giving herself to Ty, wholly and completely.

Could it be that she was ready to trust him? At least with her body? She wanted to give her sexual self to him fully and completely.

"We don't have much time," she said, desperate now for the release he promised, wishing everyone downstairs at the party would just go home and leave them alone.

Where she'd once looked at two weeks as an eternity, she now saw that it would be over in a flash.

She would miss this incredible man very, very much.

He slid her off his lap and laid her down in the middle of her old bed. He got up and locked the door, then shrugged off his blazer and draped it on the back of a chair.

He was a man on a mission, his sole purpose to make her feel good.

As a teenager, she'd fantasized about what it would be like if Ty kissed her, if he held her close. But she'd never come close to feeling this aroused, this revved up.

Then again, she'd never imagined Ty tying her up so that he could take her any way he pleased.

He walked into her closet and emerged grinning. Swinging a woven brown leather belt, he said, "This will do nicely for your wrists."

He dropped the belt beside her hip and she sucked in a breath as he undid the knot of his tie. "And this," he said, "is the perfect blindfold."

She swallowed, her mouth suddenly dry. Was she

crazy? Was she really going to let him do this to her? In her parents' house?

Drunken laughter drifted up through the floor. Didn't her parents realize that people were simply using them for free champagne and caviar, not because they actually liked them?

Perhaps being here with Ty was the perfect way to create a new, final memory in this house. After tonight, her last impression would be of a gorgeous man and the sinful things he'd done to her.

Ty sat down on the bed and his weight tilted the mattress, forcing her closer. He was warm and solid and she didn't hesitate for a second when he slid his silk tie over her eyes and reached beneath her hair to tie it.

Instantly, her remaining senses came to life. She loved his fresh, woodsy scent. The band playing "The Way We Were" downstairs sounded like the backdrop to their own personal love story. His kiss was minty on her tongue.

She suddenly saw things clearly.

All the sex, the fun, the laughter—it had been more than fooling around. She'd asked Ty to keep their relationship a secret not just because she wanted to keep her professional reputation intact, but because she was afraid that he'd turn on her, like he had before. But he wasn't a teenaged boy anymore. He was a wonderful man.

And maybe, just maybe, she thought as she reached out and laid her hand over his heart and felt its strong, steady beat, he was falling in love with her. Just like she was falling in love with him.

He wrapped his fingers around her wrist and she knew what he was going to ask.

"Only if you're sure," he said, and she smiled.

"I'm sure," she said and a moment later he had her arms secured to the bed frame, not so tight that it hurt, but just tight enough that she couldn't escape.

Heat and wetness pooled between her legs and her nipples grew hard.

"Now let's see what's waiting for me under here," Ty said, his voice and fingers coaxing a soft moan out of her as he found the zipper on the bodice of her strapless dress and pulled it open.

"You're wearing my favorite thing of all," he murmured as he slid the lace over her breasts, exposing her bare flesh all the way to her rib cage. "Nothing."

Instinctively, she arched her back, hoping he would touch her soon, kiss her, run his tongue over her nipples. He cupped her breasts with both hands and pushed them together, so that when he began to lick her, he could pay attention to both nipples at once.

She'd thought that giving her body to Ty in this way was going to be a gift for him, but it was turning out to be a gift for herself too. She'd dug out her sexiest, skimpiest panties from the back of her lingerie drawer, and tonight she was wearing just a scrap of white silk and lace beneath her white dress.

He pulled her dress over her stomach and blew out a long breath. "Every time I take your clothes off, I think I'm going to be prepared, and every time I'm wrong."

He covered her mound, silk and all, with his mouth, and his hot tongue lapped long strokes against her lips, pushed at her sex, returning again and again to her clitoris. She pulled hard against her bindings, but she couldn't break free, couldn't get close enough to his perfect mouth. Then, thank God, he pushed aside the expensive silk and slipped one thick finger inside her. His tongue met her bare flesh and he flicked it against her clit again and again, first light and then hard, then softly again.

She was desperate for release, desperate to come against his mouth. All it took was the slightest touch of his thumb and forefinger on her nipples for her orgasm to take over, from head to toe.

Before she could fall back down to earth he put his hands on her back, said, "Trust me," and shifted her wrists over each other, turning her around so that she was on her knees and shins, her breasts pressed into her bed frame.

Was this really her in bed with Ty? Blindfolded,

tied to a bed, up on her knees, waiting for him to take her? Desperate for it?

His hands were on her again, his fingers sliding against her pussy lips, her clit, slowly making their way over her stomach, the bottom of her rib cage, her breasts. Just when she didn't think she could wait another second, she felt the hot head of his penis pushing into her, stretching her wide, branding her with the feel of him.

One hard thrust was all it took for her to hit the peak again, and she rocked her ass into his pelvis, wanting to take him deeper, as deep as he could go. His hands were rough now, no longer the gentle lover. He'd given her what she'd so desperately needed, and now he was taking his pleasure in her body.

In this moment, with a belt around her wrists and a silk tie covering her eyes, Julie felt utterly complete.

She'd never think about her parents' house the same way again. And she had Ty to thank.

CHAPTER TWENTY-FOUR

An hour later, Ty nodded absently to the fan talking his ear off. He was watching Julie standing with what he guessed were family friends. Too thin, too brittle, and you could smell their unhappiness from a mile away, even though it was dressed in designer clothes.

Julie didn't look nearly as pale as she had pre-romp, but her mouth was still tight, and the tendons in her arms and neck were rigid.

He was worried about her, hoping like hell that their little romp upstairs had helped some. Ty knew with absolute certainty that she would have done the same for him, had his drunk-off-his-ass father been around.

Most of the women who came on to him were looking for not only a good time in the sack, but also a white knight to rescue them from their ordinary lives. He'd always made sure that he didn't make the mistake of getting someone pregnant, of getting into something that he couldn't easily get out of. Early on, he'd learned to look after number one. His teammates came next. There hadn't been room for anyone else.

Until now.

It was funny how fucked up everything had seemed in high school. Julie had been everything he wanted and knew he could never have, simply because they were so different.

But it turned out they weren't different after all. Because when you took away the old money and the new mansions and the trailer parks and the Super Bowl rings, all you were left with were two kids with parents who should never have signed up for the job.

Julie was the first woman he'd been with who wasn't expecting him to rescue her. And frankly, he wasn't sure she'd accept his help if he offered it.

The crazy thing was, Ty *wanted* to take care of her. He wanted her to know she could look to him for support, even if it was nothing more than two socialites who had her pinned to the wall and wouldn't let her go. There was nothing he'd rather do than drop everything and ride in to rescue her, nowhere he'd rather be.

The middle-aged man in front of him finally got to the end of his story about a game Ty'd won six years ago. Ty shook his hand. "Great talking with you. If you'll excuse me."

He kept his eyes trained on Julie as he walked across the living room, making it clear that he was temporarily off duty to the guests who were waiting to meet him.

She looked up at him a moment before he reached her side and gave him a smile that said, *"Thank God you're here."*

In that moment, Ty wanted to do more than rescue her; he wanted to claim her. Publicly. He wanted everyone to know how much she meant to him, especially her parents and their annoying, arrogant friends.

"Hello, ladies," he said smoothly as he moved next to Julie and pulled her gently against him.

She stiffened in his arms and shot him a fierce look, which he ignored. Both ladies' eyes widened in sudden comprehension and Ty swallowed the sour taste of guilt.

"We were just telling our little Julie how jealous we are that she gets to work with professional athletes. If I had known about the perks I would have gone into her line of work too." The ladies giggled like teenagers.

Ty rubbed his thumb over the sensitive skin inside Julie's elbow. She was pissed at him; he could feel it in the way she held herself.

On a positive note, though, he'd bet she wasn't thinking about her parents anymore.

Putting on his best aw-shucks voice, he said, "Jocks aren't always easy to be around. It takes one hell of an image consultant to make us look good. We're mostly thinking about our muscles and the game."

"And big breasts," Julie muttered.

One woman frowned. "Excuse me, dear, what was that you just said?"

Ty turned slightly and brushed an invisible speck off Julie's temple, which surprised her enough to keep her mouth shut for a second.

"She was saying we sweat a lot too."

Julie's blue eyes shot fire at him and he realized it was time for drastic measures. The band had just started playing a slow Sinatra tune and the dance floor was filling up.

"Excuse us. Julie promised me the first dance of the evening," he said, leading her away before she could disagree with him.

He pulled her into the center of the dance floor even though she'd made it very clear to him right from the start that she wasn't going to dance with him at parties, lest anyone misinterpret their relationship.

"What the hell are you doing?" she hissed into his ear.

"Dancing," he replied, even though he knew a smart-ass reply would just wind her up more.

A muffled curse reverberated against his chest. "People are looking at us. Getting ideas."

He pulled her closer and inhaled the scent of their lovemaking that clung to her skin. His cock reared up in his pants.

"I know. Let 'em look."

She looked at him, and where he expected anger, he saw confusion instead.

He wanted to say something that would help her understand where he was coming from. Only problem was, he couldn't figure out how to string a coherent sentence together. Not when her curves were pressed against him and he was ready to run back upstairs for high-school-fantasy-night, part two.

"Ty," she said softly, "everyone is going to think we're together. You're acting like I'm your girlfriend, not a hired consultant."

Ty couldn't go on playing this game anymore. He wanted her. She wanted him. It was time for them to be together. For real.

"Then they're thinking right."

She sucked in a breath and two spots of red colored her cheekbones. "We had an agreement. This thing is supposed to be a secret. No strings, right?"

She pushed out of his arms and waded through the guests. He followed close behind her, out the

French doors, down the steps, past a pond, onto a path that lead through a thick hedge.

When they were far away from everyone else, he reached for her and spun her around. She was breathing hard and her anger was alive between them.

"How dare you?" she spat. "You of all people should know how hard it is for me to be here, in my parents' house, with everyone watching me. After what you just did, everyone is going to be talking about how sad it is that I let myself have a crush on you, the big superstar. That you'll dump me cold at the first sight of a new pair of overinflated breasts."

She slapped his hands away from her waist.

"Ever since I've been working with you, I've barely been maintaining my professional reputation. Do you want me to have to start all over again? Is that what this is all about?"

His heart thudded in his chest. She was dead wrong about him. About his motives.

"I love you."

Her eyes grew big and he knew she needed to hear it again. And he needed to say it again, to let the truth sink into his bones.

"I love you, Julie."

She stumbled back a step, sat down hard on a stone bench, and he kneeled at her feet. She wouldn't look at him. He held her cold hands between his.

"I know we had an agreement," he admitted. "But things have changed."

She lifted her chin, blinked at him. "How? How have they changed? You're still you and I'm still me."

He moved to sit next to her on the bench. "At first we were playing a game of cat and mouse. We both wanted to see who would win. But that's not where we are anymore."

"Just because you like having sex with me doesn't mean you love me."

"I've liked having sex with lots of people."

Her eyes shot fire at him again. "Thanks for the reminder."

"But I haven't loved any of them." He brushed his thumb across her lower lip. "Just you."

She leaned into his hand the slightest bit, and the vise grip around Ty's heart eased up.

"You've caught me off guard," she whispered. "I don't know what to think."

He pulled her onto his lap, then pressed a gentle kiss to her lips. "Trust me," he said against her soft mouth "We're going to be great together."

✳

Julie's head was spinning. It was just like Ty to spring the word *love* on her. One minute he was helping her forget all of her old fears, and the next, so many new doubts were piling on top of each other.

What about how deeply he'd hurt her before?

What about the throngs of beautiful women who waited for him at every game, outside his locker room, and on the lounge chairs around his swimming pool?

For so long, she'd held herself back from pleasure because she'd been so afraid of being hurt again. What if this was her one and only chance to really be happy?

Maybe it was time to take a chance—to let herself be with a man who said he loved her. And then, if things continued to go well—if he didn't leave her and she didn't lose all of her business because everyone thought she was a sucker for falling for a rich playboy quarterback—maybe she could even tell him how much she'd always loved him.

But for now, she'd just let herself fall into the net he was offering. All she knew for sure was that she loved the feel of his strong arms around her, his muscular thighs beneath hers. Just sitting on his lap made her wet and hungry for him.

She said, "Love me, Ty," and it seemed like she'd hardly drawn a breath before he'd repositioned her with her dress up around her hips and her legs wrapped around his waist.

His fingers moved between them and she loved the way his knuckles brushed and teased her clit as his undid his zipper and pulled his cock free. A fresh wave of arousal flooded her as he slid on a condom, the thick head of his hard-on less than an inch from her pussy lips.

And then he was sliding inside of her, huge and thick and hot. His hands were on her ass, pulling her up on his cock and then back down, harder and faster. She rode the long wave of her budding orgasm, everything inside of her wanting to believe he loved her.

That he would always love her.

As his thumb found her clitoris, he pushed her up and over the crest, and whispered, "I love you."

The words lingered in her head long after her climax had subsided.

CHAPTER TWENTY-FIVE

Julie barely registered her phone ringing the following morning as Ty stirred beneath her, mumbling something about leaving the damn phone off the hook from now on. She felt so wonderful with her head cradled in the crook of his arm, his heartbeat rhythmic and soothing in her ear.

But after years of being the ultimate professional, she couldn't ignore the telephone. What if there was a fire she needed to put out for one of her clients?

And what, the warning voice in her head asked in a much louder voice, if the fire was in her own bed?

Suddenly Julie was wide awake.

She scooted up in bed and pulled the duvet up over her naked breasts. She knew it was ridiculous, that no one but Ty could see her right now. Still, as she reached for the phone she brushed her hair back from her eyes and straightened her spine.

"Julie Spencer," she said in as crisp a voice as she could manage on approximately three hours of sleep.

"Honey, I'm so happy for you!"

Julie's mother had never called her this early in the morning. Usually, she was in bed until late morning, due to one drink too many.

Fear shot up Julie's spine. What was going on?

"Thanks, Mother," she said in a falsely calm voice. "Do you mind my asking what you're so happy about?"

Her mother sighed. "Oh Julie, you always did hold your cards too close to your chest."

Julie didn't say anything, just waited for her mother to get to the point.

"You found your prince charming, sweetie! None of my friends can stop talking about how gorgeous he is. And the way he looks at you makes me wish I was young and beautiful again."

This was the point where Julie would have usually said something like, "You're still beautiful, Mother," but today the words just weren't there.

"It's no big deal," she said, wishing her mother wouldn't get so excited about her budding relationship with Ty. If things between them didn't work out, she didn't want to have to console her mother in addition to herself.

"Every mother wants to see her daughter fall in

love with a strong, wonderful man. Not to mention filthy rich. I can't wait to see more of Ty!"

Her mother's giggle grated on Julie's sleep-deprived nerves, but before she could figure out a civil, nice-daughter response, her call waiting beeped.

"I've got a work call on the other line, Mother. I have to go." Julie clicked over.

"Good morning Miss Spencer," came Bobby's slow drawl. "I hear you're taking special care of my number one boy."

Oh, God. "Ty's been doing great," she said in as crisp and professional a voice as she could manage, considering her client's "number one boy" was in her bed.

Ty looked at her from beneath the arm over his eyes. "Who is it?" He sounded sleepy, lazy, and utterly unconcerned.

She shook her head, put her finger over her lips, and mouthed, "Bobby."

Ty shifted onto his hip and the sheets slid from his torso, leaving a mouthwatering expanse of his skin and muscle.

"Who?"

She covered the mouth piece tighter. "Shh!" But it was too late.

"Now isn't this convenient? The two people I want to talk to are already gathered in one room."

"Bobby, I—" she began, but Ty had already

bounded up out of the bed and grabbed the extension in her office next door.

"Hey, boss. You need something this fine morning?"

Ty's drawl was a match for Bobby's, even without the thick southern accent.

Julie felt like she was going to throw up. Or hyperventilate.

"You and your pretty lady just sit tight. I'll be right over."

Julie's mouth opened. Then closed. Finally, she pushed a "Wonderful" out just before Bobby hung up on them both.

She flew out of the bed. "Fuck, fuck, fuck!"

Ty stood against the doorframe. "I never thought I'd hear you say that word once, let alone three times." He raked his gaze up, then down, her bare skin. "And it's a bonus that you're naked."

Julie growled, then dashed into the bathroom. She threw her hair up into a bun and walked into a wall of cold water.

"Shit, shit, shit!"

Of course she'd figured people would be interested in finding out more about her, the woman who had captured Ty's heart. She'd planned on setting up a meeting with Bobby first thing Monday morning to present her revised plan for the final week of her contract. But she'd gotten so caught up in Ty's "I love you" that the part of her brain that had always put her business first had stopped functioning altogether.

In typical Ty fashion, he waited until steam started to rise from the shower to get in. Julie dropped the soap and then her razor. She couldn't stop shaking.

"Everything's going to be fine," Ty said.

"What do you care?" she accused. "You're not going to be fired."

He shrugged. "Isn't that why they hired you? To turn me into a good boy so they wouldn't have to fire my ass?"

She flipped off the tap and roughly dried herself off with a towel. Ty gently took it from her.

"Why don't you let me do that, before you scar that gorgeous skin of yours?"

What was she going to say to Bobby about her relationship with Ty? How could she possibly spin things so it looked like she was still doing her job? Because quite frankly, Julie wasn't at all sure that she was anymore.

Having sex countless times a day with a hot pro football player definitely wasn't listed by the IRS as "gainful employment."

"Now look," Ty said in a voice meant to calm her. "We haven't done anything wrong. You've worked your fine ass off to reform me, and even from my perspective I can see that you've done a fine job."

She wasn't in a smiling mood, but it was nice

hearing that she'd been successful at taming a wild mustang, straight from the horse's mouth.

"I don't recall seeing any contract that said you and I couldn't date."

She bit her lip. "True."

"Being with a successful, beautiful woman like you makes a guy like me look good. Bobby's not stupid, even if he pretends he is. He'll see that my being with a babe like you is an asset."

Julie wasn't sure what was worse. The fact that the man she was relying on to pay a boatload of her bills was about to pound on her door, or that her boyfriend was a jerk who actually referred to her as "a babe like you."

She spun away and reached for the first thing in her closet. What the hell had she been thinking being with a guy like Ty? Then she realized he was chuckling.

"Can't you take anything seriously for one second?" she yelled.

"Admit it," he said, "you're not thinking about Bobby anymore, are you?"

She shoved him on the bed. "So all that 'your fine ass' and 'babe, you're an asset' stuff was merely a ploy to take my mind off of this horrible situation? You didn't say it because you're stuck in the fifties and can't stop picturing me in the kitchen with an apron on?"

"Better I'm with you than a stripper, right?"

Julie dragged a comb through her hair. She hated that he was right, hated that she was exactly the kind of woman she would have set Ty up with.

She'd brushed mascara over her pale lashes just as the doorbell rang.

"I'll get it," Ty said, walking through her house as if he owned it.

Julie let him go. If ever there was a morning for bright red lipstick, this was it.

She emerged from her bedroom just as Ty opened the door.

"They've got great coffee on the corner, don't they?" Ty greeted his team's owner.

"I'll have to come back another time and find out."

"I'll brew a pot," Julie said, gesturing for Bobby to take the plush seat facing the park.

Bobby waved away her offer. "A lovely offer, but unnecessary. Why don't you both sit down."

Julie was amazed by how quickly Bobby took control of everyone around him. She felt like an intruder in her own house, like she should see herself out when he was done reading her the riot act.

She sat down on the hardest chair in her living room and primly crossed her legs, keeping her expression warm but closed. She wasn't stupid enough to frame herself for high crimes and misdemeanors. Ty, of course, flopped down on her sofa and kicked his legs up.

Not a care in the world, that was always his game.

Bobby looked utterly at ease. "It's come to my attention," he said, "that you are no longer a man about town, Ty."

Ty grinned. "Julie's making an honest man out of me."

Julie bit down on the inside of her lip. Anything she'd say now would only make it worse. Maybe if she just sat here and smiled, everything would play out fine between Ty and his boss.

And maybe cows would start flying soon.

"Hard to believe a smart gal like you would fall for a pro ballplayer," he said to her. "Especially my number one boy over here."

"You must not know Ty very well," she retorted, unable to toe the party line for the first time in her career. "He's more than just a ballplayer. More than just a commodity."

Bobby looked back and forth between the two of them and smiled widely.

"True love is a blessed thing."

Julie glanced at Ty, shocked to find him nodding, even though he'd sworn his love to her just twelve hours ago.

"Sure is," he said and Julie forced herself to smile.

Bobby stood up. "I feel much better about everything now that I've confirmed the rumors about the two of you."

Julie stood and smoothed her skirt, more than happy to see Bobby to the door. That hadn't been bad at all. He hadn't yelled at her or fired her.

He stepped out into the hallway, then turned to face her with one final thought.

"But I hired you to clean up my boy's reputation, not to use him as your personal boy toy. Couldn't be better timing, making an honest man out of him before the season starts. I'll expect to see the announcement of your engagement ASAP."

Julie watched him walk away, trying to catch her breath.

In one short week, her entire world had imploded. Then again, she'd never been in such an intense relationship, one that overshadowed everything else.

The last thing she expected to see upon returning inside was Ty on her living room carpet doing an impossibly fast set of push-ups. She'd watched him work out in the gym for a week now, but he'd never moved with such intensity and speed.

He was panting loudly and his shirt was soaked with sweat, but he didn't let up, didn't stop moving even though his lungs and muscles had to be on fire.

Sweet Lord, he was the sexiest thing to ever drip on her carpet.

Ty glanced up at her. "Ninety-eight. Ninety-nine. One hundred." He rolled over onto his back and curled his legs into his chest as he sucked in air. "I'm afraid the push-ups didn't work. I'm still going to have to kill the bastard."

Julie had to ask, even though she didn't really want to know the answer. "Why?"

Ty rolled out of the fetal position and grabbed her hand, pulling her down on the rug with him.

"I don't give a shit if he treats me like a two-year-old. But like hell if he's going to ever disrespect you again."

Julie shook her head. "It doesn't bother me," she lied. "Sometimes clients like to feel like they're smarter than you, like they have the upper hand. It's no big deal."

But it was. Julie never would have put up with this kind of treatment from anyone else. The worst part was, deep down she knew exactly why she was letting herself play doormat: because the only other choice—resigning from the account with her pride intact—wasn't a choice at all.

Not if it meant sending Ty back to his old life and returning to hers.

"We're not going to get married because some power-hungry ass wipe told us to," he said.

Julie tilted her head down, stared at a piece of lint and worked like hell to fight back the sudden tears pooling behind her eyes.

"Of course we're not. He's just talking crazy."

They weren't going to get married. Not this week or next year. She knew that, had always known it. So why was she getting so upset about it?

Ty ripped off his damp shirt, balled it up, and threw it on the coffee table.

"I'm saying this all wrong, Julie."

Desperate to lighten the tension in the room, she said, "You did the right thing, not killing him. I don't know how much football they let you play in prison."

He grinned, but it was gone in a flash. "I don't give a crap about football right now. We need to talk about us. About getting married."

Her breath caught in her throat.

"When I ask you to marry me, it sure as hell isn't gong to be because my boss made me."

When I ask you to marry me?

Thank God she was sitting down.

"You and I need to settle this, figure out what we're doing," Ty continued. "Bobby's right about one thing: We need a game plan."

He was right. They needed a game plan not only for their private relationship, but their public one as well.

She needed to start working things out on paper. Which media outlets to call, which writer to give an exclusive to, an emergency meeting with her staff to fill them in and let them know the official comment.

She jumped up. "Before you or I talk to anyone else, I need to draft a press release and get it out."

Ty smiled. "Looks like the image consultant I love has found her way back into the building."

"I'll be in my office." How could she have forgotten for one second that she had the skills to turn things around? "Be sure to make a list of everyone who leaves you a phone message this morning."

Ty grabbed an OJ out of the fridge, his cell phone up to his ear as he checked his voice mails. "Strange days when people go crazy about me dating a nice girl," he said.

In any other case, Julie would have agreed. But she was no ordinary nice girl, just like he was no regular bad boy.

CHAPTER TWENTY-SIX

Ty punched in his voice mail access code. He hadn't recognized the number on the screen, but he wouldn't put it past most of the journalists he knew to call for a firsthand scoop on his new relationship.

The canned voice said, "You have three messages," and he took a long swig of juice. He was looking for a pen to start making Julie a list when he realized a kid was talking, not an adult.

"Um, hi, this is a message for Ty. He said I could call him if I needed to. This is Jack, from camp. I really need to talk to him."

Message two: "Um, I really need to talk to Ty. Bad. This is Jack from camp. I'm in big trouble."

Message three was mostly sniffles along with, "This is Jack again and I'm at the hospital in Palo Alto and I really need Ty. They told me I can't call him again."

Ty scrolled through his cell phone's menu to access the number Jake had called him from, but it was listed as "Withheld."

He grabbed a clean shirt and jammed it into his jeans, then stepped into Julie's office.

"I gotta go."

She barely looked up from her computer.

"You can't. Not until I send this out and we go over our official press statement."

"That kid from camp, Jack, is in the hospital in Palo Alto. I told him to call me if he needed help. He called. I'll bet they can't find his drunk-ass dad."

Julie stood up. "I'm coming with you."

"I don't need a babysitter. I'm not going to do anything that'll get more bad press."

"I know you don't need a babysitter," she said in such a gentle voice that Ty felt like a jerk. "I was thinking you might need a girlfriend instead."

He pulled her into his arms. "I'm sorry. I didn't mean it."

"I know you didn't." She pressed a kiss onto his lips. "Let's go."

*

The thirty-minute drive felt more like three days, and Ty got some insight into what it must be like to be a parent. He hoped like hell that Jack was okay and that his father hadn't already shown up to make things worse.

Inside the hospital, Julie scanned the map on the wall. "Let's check pediatrics first."

He followed Julie onto the elevator, keeping his head down. No eye contact with strangers was crucial; he didn't have time to sign autographs and bullshit about football.

Jack was sitting in a blue chair in the corner of the pediatric waiting room, his head hung so low his chest was crammed up against his chest.

"Hey, buddy."

Jack looked up at the sound of his voice, then he wiped away a tear running down his cheek.

"You came."

"I'm always around to help out a friend." He let go of Julie's hand and took the too-small seat next to Jack. "What's up?"

"Nothing, I guess. I was playing with some guys in the neighborhood and sprained my wrist. The doctor said I could go home." His head fell back to his chest. "I thought I broke it, but I guess the sound I heard was just the other guy's helmet hitting mine."

Inwardly, Ty winced. "Hurts like hell, huh?"

He knew the drill with sprains. Lots of pain, no sympathy, and you were expected to get right back out there on the field.

Jack shrugged, playing tough guy.

"They said I should take these every four hours." He held up a sample bottle of children's Motrin.

Ty leaned forward on his knees. "You hungry?"

Jack nodded. "Starved."

"I know a place that makes great burgers. Used to go there after games."

For the first time since they'd walked into the waiting room, Jack's eyes lit up.

"You're not taking me straight home?"

Ty looked the kid in the eye. "You haven't told your dad yet?"

Jack shook his head. "He's going to be really mad."

Jack's dad was going to shit a brick at the thought of his little prizewinner's future possibly getting screwed up. Ty was pretty sure Jack's days of neighborhood pickup games were over.

"First we'll eat lunch. Then we'll tell him. Together."

Julie stood up. "I'll let the nurse know we're heading out."

The first sign that Jack was feeling better was the endless chatter that filled first the waiting room, then the car, and then their booth in the back of The Boardwalk, a burger and pizza dive that had survived the endless Silicon Valley boom.

But rather than feeling better about everything now that Jack clearly was on the mend, what had happened with Jack hit too close to home. Way too close.

All week at football camp, Ty'd had the uncomfortable sensation that he'd been stepping into his past. He could guess what Jack's life was like: teachers pushing him into the next grade whether he'd earned it or not, never having to be accountable for screwing up on or off the field simply because everyone—coaches, his drunk-ass dad, girlfriends, even his buddies—wanted a piece of his success.

Ty could see into Jack's future. He'd go to college for the exposure, not an education, and he'd quit the minute a seven-figure deal landed in his lap.

From that point forward, he'd live in fear of getting hurt. Later, when he had more money than he knew what to do with, he might break down and hire some secret tutors to teach him all the things he'd missed along the way, like reading and science and an appreciation for something other than football.

Was he just as bad as everyone else in Jack's life? After all, wasn't he on the verge of sending Jack back home after making some excuses to his father about how accidents happened, and not to worry? Ty had never thought of himself as a chicken shit.

Until now.

Turning to Julie, he said, "Jack and I need to talk outside for a few minutes, man to man. You don't mind, do you?"

She smiled at them both. "Take as long as you need. I'll just sit here and work on my French fries."

Jack followed him out of the restaurant and they sat down on a bench just outside the window. Julie munched on fries and pretended not to look at them.

He'd never known a woman could be like her. Soft and warm, yet hard when she needed to be. A dozen times smarter than anyone he knew, and at the same time sexier than hell.

Jack kicked a rock off the sidewalk. "You wanna go over what we're going to tell my dad, so he doesn't get too pissed?"

Ty focused on Jack's expensive sneakers. Nothing but the best equipment for this kid, whether he deserved it or not. Unfortunately, if he didn't lay down some hard truths and set Jack straight, no one ever would. Everyone else had too much to gain from Jack's eventual success.

"I was a lot like you when I was a kid."

"Really? Cool."

"My dad was pretty messed up a lot of the time. Still is, actually."

"Did he freak when you got hurt?"

"Sure did. All he cared about was whether I could play in the next game, or if the injury would affect my future. I acted like I wasn't in pain, even when I was." He paused. "Is your arm still throbbing?"

Jack nodded. "A little." He swallowed. "A lot, actually. But I don't want my dad to know."

Ty had a feeling he was screwing this up. Big-time. "You got any hobbies? Something besides football?"

"You mean like my Xbox 360?"

Ty grinned. "Not exactly. I was just wondering if you like to read or build things."

"My dad says I'm supposed to focus on football. He says it's going to make us rich."

It was going to take every ounce of Ty's self-control to keep from rearranging Jack's father's face.

"Maybe. Maybe not. Getting rich in football depends on a lot of things."

Jack frowned, probably because it was the first time anyone had ever told him fame and fortune wasn't a sure thing. "Like what? I've got the skills."

"You do. But things happen. You could get drafted onto a Super Bowl–winning team."

Jack smirked like he already knew that was going to happen.

"Or you could get hurt, like some of the super-talented guys I knew in high school and college, and your career could end." He snapped his fingers. "Just like that."

Jack thrust his chin out. "That didn't happen to you. You're a huge star."

"I'm one of the lucky ones," Ty said, even as he wondered if he really was. "And I worry about getting hurt, about being taken out on a stretcher, every single game."

When he was younger and felt completely invincible, he'd never worried about the end of his career. But now, guys he'd played with since his rookie days were starting to retire. The ones with a plan for retirement did fine. But the guys who didn't have a single dream other than football just plain fell apart.

"Don't you have enough money to do whatever you want?"

"Sure," Ty conceded. "But money isn't everything."

Until Julie had come back into his life, Ty couldn't see the point in anything but football. Now he had new ideas. He'd just started thinking maybe one day he could open his own summer camp in Grass Valley, maybe for kids like him who didn't have money for fancy shoes and trust funds. They'd play football, but they'd learn other stuff too. Like fishing and how to start a campfire. Ty wanted to run the idea by Julie, see what she thought.

"Your life has to be about more than football, kid," Ty said, deciding it was time to get straight to the point. "It doesn't matter if everyone else treats you like a god. One day someone is going to come along who shows you what a screwup you really are. And you're not going to be able to fix it, because the only thing you'll know how to do is play football."

Jack didn't say anything and he wasn't making eye contact anymore.

"I'm not trying to make you feel bad," Ty said. "And I'll still talk to your dad. I just want you to think about what I'm saying."

Jack jumped off the bench. "I'm going to be the greatest football player in history! I'm going to leave you in the dust. You don't know anything!"

Julie ran outside. "What's happening? Is your arm hurting, Jack? Do you need to see the doctor again?"

Ty had never seen such a hard face on a little kid. Except maybe his own in the mirror.

"I want to go home," Jack whined.

Julie nodded and gave him her keys. "Go ahead and wait in the car. I need to talk to Ty for a sec."

She turned on him. "What did you say to him? He looked like he was about to cry."

Ty willed her to understand. "Trust me, it was stuff he needed to hear."

"He's just a little boy, Ty. You hurt his feelings."

"I had my reasons for what I said to the kid."

"Go ahead," she said, her eyes challenging him. "Tell me your reasons. I'm dying to hear them."

But everything was hitting too close to home. He didn't want to talk about it right now, didn't want to bare his soul in front of a restaurant with Jack waiting in the parking lot.

"Don't push me," he growled. Julie needed to back off long enough for him to get a grip.

Her expression went from concerned to confused to cold in a millisecond. "You know what? I
can't think of one single reason you could have for
making a sweet little boy cry."

"Not even one, huh?"

Everything in him wanted to get down on his
knees and explain the truth to her, that things weren't
how she thought they were. But he'd done that before
and it hadn't made a lick of difference. Julie had her
mind made up. He was guilty as charged.

She moved toward him, her cheeks red, her blue
eyes full of anger. "I was so stupid I actually thought
you'd changed. That you could be a man for once,
instead of the self-absorbed little boy you always were."

A slow anger began to burn inside of Ty, a fire
stoked by every person who had ever doubted he
could be more than a football player, by everyone
who'd thought they could take advantage of a poor
dumb kid like him.

"You want to know why your dates aren't interested in you, babe?" He watched the word *babe* hit
her across the face like a hard slap, along with more
he didn't mean, but somehow couldn't stop from saying. "Because guys don't like the third degree. You
can't run a relationship like a business. And it's time
to get it into your pretty little head that what went
down between me and Jack is none of your damn
business."

He'd never been able to forget the look on Julie's face on the yacht when she'd said, "I hate you." Here it was again.

"Your image is no longer any concern of mine," she said. Then, just in case he wasn't clear that she was severing both their professional *and* personal relationships, she added, "I'll send your things by courier by this afternoon."

He watched her walk across the parking lot, get in her car, and drive away. Just hours ago she was naked on his lap. Now she was telling him what a worthless asshole he was. As if his father hadn't drummed that into his head every time he blew it on the field his entire childhood.

His phone rang. "What?"

Jay's voice boomed out of the earpiece. "Got a couple of things to discuss this fine morning."

"Make it quick," Ty growled.

"Care to confirm a serious relationship with a pretty blonde?"

"Negative." Even if it killed him to say it, he was going to get the words out. "We were just having fun. We're done now."

"Got it," Jay said, moving smoothly onto his second order of business. "Looks like one of the biggest companies in the world wants your name and face attached to their product."

"Whatever," Ty said, not in the mood to deal with

business right now. "As long as the money's good, I'm in."

Jay was uncharacteristically silent for a moment. "Great! I told them you wouldn't have any problem with the product."

A warning bell went off. "What is it?"

"I know how you feel about alcohol, and you know the League won't let players promote it anyway, so that's one big moneymaker that's always had a red *X* through it. But I've found the next big thing and they want you to be their man."

He paused for effect, and Ty suddenly wondered why he hadn't found a new agent a long time ago.

"Buzzed Cola is going to pay you ten million dollars to do worldwide print and TV advertising for one year!"

Ty didn't need the money and he wasn't a huge fan of the new ultra-caffeine drink that everyone swigged like water. He knew exactly why the advertisers wanted him on board. As soon as kids saw him drinking Buzzed Cola, they'd be lining up to buy cases of it. Ten minutes ago, he would have said no without giving it a second thought.

Then again, ten minutes ago Julie hadn't looked at him like he was the scum of the earth.

Ten minutes ago, he thought that maybe, just maybe she was going to love him back.

Too bad he was such an idiot. Julie was never

going to stop thinking of him as a fuck-up. And right now Ty couldn't think of a single reason not to act like one.

"I'll think about it," he said, hanging up on his agent and calling a local cab company. "Hey, I need a ride from Palo Alto to San Francisco." He nearly gave Julie's address, before he remembered he wasn't welcome there anymore. It was time to go back to his overinflated excuse for a home.

Alone.

CHAPTER TWENTY-SEVEN

As a young child, Julie had mastered the art of numbing her emotions. She'd block out her mother's drunken scenes, she'd convince herself that her father's mistresses really were her nannies, just like he said. All of that practice came in handy as she drove Jack home on autopilot. She tried to go inside the beautiful stucco two-story house with him, but he barely let her hit the brakes before he jumped out of the backseat and ran through a side gate into his backyard.

Still, she missed his small, angry presence once he was gone and she was left sitting in her car, staring at the empty passenger seat that Ty had curled his tall, muscular body into for the past two weeks.

Ty's final words played on repeat inside her brain; *"none of your damn business"* jostling for first place on the leaderboard of shame with *"You want to know why your dates aren't interested in you, babe?"*

Even though she'd known all along that she was nothing special to him, that a guy like him couldn't possibly know the true meaning of the word *love*, she hadn't thought she would feel so much pain when he finally showed his true colors.

Julie drove back to the city, but before she went home, she needed to make an important pit stop. This time she was going to be the one to walk away first, to cut every single tie that bound them together.

She walked into the Outlaws headquarters and had security buzz Bobby. A guy like him worked 24-7 and she had a hunch she'd find him in his office, making his way through a list of the people whose lives he planned to ruin now that he'd finished with her.

"Bobby Wilson here."

"It's Julie Spencer. I need a word. Now."

She had to give him points for how quickly he masked his surprise. "I can always spare a moment for a pretty lady such as yourself."

Julie ground her teeth together. God, she hated being called "pretty lady" every other sentence. Maybe it was time to take some kickboxing lessons. That way she could knock the teeth out of the next guy who acted like she was a Thoroughbred for sale.

His door was open when she got off the elevator.

"Now, what can I do for you, my dear?"

She smiled sweetly. "I quit."

He raised his eyebrows in surprise. "Are you referring to your job with my boy Ty?"

Julie wanted to tell Bobby that Ty was irredeemable. She wanted to say that there was no point in hiring another image consultant or PR agency to replace her, because working with Ty was an impossible task. But even in her current state, she knew those were the rantings of a woman done wrong.

Worse, they made her sound pathetic and lovelorn, something she swore she'd never be again.

"I'm afraid I took your client on under false pretenses. I had never worked with a professional athlete before and it turns out that an assignment like this is beyond the boundaries of my expertise. You will not be receiving an invoice from my company for the work already done."

Bobby sat back in his chair, then tilted his cowboy hat back on his shiny bald head. "Trouble in paradise?"

She refused to react to his taunting. But she wasn't going to lie either and say that she and Ty hadn't been an item; even though they hadn't lasted twenty-four hours in the public eye.

"Ty Calhoun and I are not a couple. And from this point on, he is no longer my client. Good luck with the team."

CHAPTER TWENTY-EIGHT

I shouldn't have resigned from the Outlaws account without talking it over with you first. I've put the entire company at risk," Julie said bitterly.

Amy sat next to Julie on the couch in her office and rubbed her back. "I should never have let you take the assignment. Not after what you told me about your past."

Julie shook her head. "I needed the money. For the stupid building." Damn her pride for not billing Bobby for the time she'd put in. She was screwed. "I don't know how I'm going to pay the mortgage and everyone's salaries. I'm so sorry."

"If you're waiting for me to tell you that you did the wrong thing, forget it. Sometimes your principles have to come first. Besides," Amy added, "you did a great job. Ty was photographed at charity events, fund-raisers, and as a coach at a children's camp, plus he was the subject of several great, feel-good feature stories. You virtually eradicated his image as a good-for-nothing bad boy overnight. We're bound to get some great new clients."

Julie wished her friend's praise could make her feel better. But not only was her business on the verge of ruin, she felt hollow and cold. She had to figure out a way to stop loving Ty. Because even though he was a selfish bastard, she still couldn't stop thinking about him.

What if ten years of longing stretched into twenty?

What if she never got over him?

The only way she knew how to forget Ty was to bury herself in work. It had almost worked before. And until she could figure out another tactic, work was all she had.

Julie typed in her email password and let herself be buried beneath a flood of queries and demands that suddenly seemed utterly meaningless.

＊

No matter how Ty tried to fill them, there were too many hours in the day. He got up early to sweat away his demons in the gym, he stayed late with the new round of kids at Tony's football camp, and ran for miles along the cliffs near his house.

During the week he'd been at Julie's, his housekeeping staff told him the all-day parties had whittled away, leaving his house empty and silent as a tomb. Ty couldn't see the point in inviting his buddies back over, in having a bunch of bikini-clad women in his backyard anymore. And he definitely couldn't head down those steps beneath his garage and not revisit that first potent kiss, the one that proved ten years hadn't dulled their passion for each other in the least.

Thank God training camp started next Monday. He just needed to make it through the rest of the week, then he could bury his feelings in football and ice packs and strategy sessions.

For a couple of days he'd actually considered doing the Buzzed Cola ads. But spite and pride were damn stupid reasons for advocating something he despised.

He closed his eyes to get through his next set on the bench press, and when he opened them Dominic was standing behind him, spotting.

"Benching three hundred pounds isn't the smartest thing in the world to be doing by yourself," Dominic said.

"Gotta get ready for pre-season."

Dom nodded. "I'm glad you're here, actually. I wanted to chat for a minute."

Ty dragged his sorry ass over to the pull-up bar. "Shoot."

"I've been hearing things about your agent. Have been for some time, actually."

Ty wished he could say he was surprised, but he wasn't. He'd been putting off dealing with Jay for way too long.

"Probably time to find a new agent."

Dom nodded. "Good plan." He paused for a moment, then caught Ty's eyes in the mirror behind the free weights. "You let me know if you need anything, okay? Wouldn't want you to drop three hundred pounds on your ribs."

Ty appreciated Dom's none-too-subtle offer. "Will do," he said, heading for the showers. It was time to take care of some overdue business.

*

All Julie wanted was a quiet evening at home to catch up on her emails. She was going to brew a pot of tea, put on her most comfortable sweats, and sit on the couch with her computer on her lap until she'd cleared out her inbox. She'd just put the kettle on when her cell phone rang.

She wasn't going to answer it, but when her mother's private number flashed on the screen, Julie's efficient evening flew out the window. Her mother called for only one reason: because she was sick from drink and no one else was willing to help her.

"Oh Julie, I'm so glad you're home. I have the stomach flu again. Estella can't stay the night."

Julie heard her mother's assistant in the background saying, "You need to get back into bed, Carol."

Thirty minutes later, Julie entered her mother's private wing. The lights had been dimmed and the room smelled like rum and vomit.

The last time Julie had been in her parents' house, Ty had been with her. He'd been so loving that night, so attuned to not only her embarrassment, but also the discomfort that wrapped around her whenever she set foot in this house.

She didn't want to think about him, didn't want to give him any credit—but if he'd been there for her when she needed him, why would he have turned on a scared little boy?

All week, an insistent little voice had been saying, *Maybe you were wrong. Maybe you should have listened to Ty's side of the story.*

Her mother was lying against a stack of pillows, groaning. "Julie, is that you?"

She sat down on the bed. "How are you feeling?"

"Horrible. I must have had some bad seafood again."

Julie nodded, even though she knew damn well that salmonella had nothing whatsoever to do with her mother's predicament. Everyone knew Carol was an alcoholic, but no one had the nerve to tell her to take hold of her life and get some help.

Julie's heart squeezed tight in her chest as she finally faced a truth that had been nearly thirty years in coming: She'd never been brave enough to face her own personal demons, either.

And yet she'd expected Ty to come clean and face all of his in the public eye.

And he had. Ty didn't lie about cutting ties with his alcoholic father, a man who had refused treatment time and time again, even though it would have been on Ty's dime.

Sure, Ty had gotten swept up in the money and the fame that came with being a pro athlete. But at least he'd been honest about where he'd come from.

Whereas she'd spent her whole life hiding behind the facade of perfection, in both her personal and business lives. It wasn't right to expect Ty to change if she wouldn't step up to the plate and deal with her own big problems.

Julie stood up and started opening the thick drapes one by one. The sun hadn't yet set and the sky was a clear, beautiful blue.

"Too bright!" her mother complained, but Julie ignored her.

"Where's Daddy tonight?"

Her mother grimaced and covered her eyes with her hand. "He's got a late business meeting."

Julie grabbed her phone out of her purse and dialed her father's cell. "This is your daughter, Julie. I'll be at your office in fifteen minutes. You and I need to have a quick chat."

Carol sat up in bed, knocking off several pillows. "What are you doing?"

"What I should have done a long time ago. Whatever relationship you and my father have agreed to is none of my business, but I'm not a little girl anymore and I'm not going to act like one. You don't really have the stomach flu."

Carol went completely white. "What are you talking about? Of course I do."

Julie moved to the bed and took her mother's hands into her own. "You can't keep doing this to yourself. Drinking has never solved any of your problems. Please, let me help you."

Carol's tears fell onto the back of Julie's hand. "I don't know if can."

Julie smiled. "I love you, Mom. You're a strong woman. We both are."

"All I ever wanted was for you to be happy." Julie knew one of the reasons her mother had stayed with her father was because she thought it was the best thing for Julie. "Are you happy, honey?"

Julie took a deep breath. "I'm getting there." She

kissed her mother on the forehead. "I'll talk to you tomorrow, okay? We'll make some plans."

Her father was sitting behind his massive mahogany desk when she arrived. His "assistant" was the only other person in the office, and Julie was certain that she'd interrupted a night out on the town.

"I don't like being given orders, Julie," her father said.

Julie walked over to the window along the back wall, watching the sun setting over the Bay.

More than anything, she wanted to see Ty again and beg for his forgiveness for being such a cold, judgmental bitch. But first she had to own up to her life's loose ends.

"The apple doesn't fall far from the tree," she said, her back to her father. Some of his faults resided within her: his pride, his stubbornness. They'd helped her build a business, but they'd nearly destroyed her personal life.

"If this is about you breaking up with that football player, go cry to your mother about it. I'm a busy man."

Julie turned to face her father. How nice to know he cared. "But not too busy to sleep with your assistant on a regular basis, right?"

Blake's face turned a nasty shade of red. "You know nothing whatsoever about my personal life."

She nodded. "You're right. I don't. Because you've never shared one single thing with me."

He pushed his chair back. "We're through here."

She moved toward him, steady and confident in front of him for the first time. She felt different on the inside. Sure, she'd always displayed an outer confidence, but it no longer felt like it was just a part she was playing to get ahead, to win clients and money. "Not quite."

Unaccustomed to the powerful woman standing before him, Blake sat back down.

"I came here to tell you that Mom has agreed to enter a treatment program for her alcoholism, and if you do one single thing to throw her off course, you'll regret it." She forced her lips into a farce of a smile. "Good night. Have a nice date."

It wasn't until she got behind the wheel of her car that she realized that her hands were shaking.

Now only two items were left on her to-do list. Figure out a way to save her business and convince Ty to give her another chance.

CHAPTER TWENTY-NINE

Ty walked into his agent's posh office unan-
nounced. By the time Jay's pretty young assistant figured out how to operate the intercom, Ty
had already made himself comfortable on Jay's suede
guest chair. Quickly masking his surprise, Jay flicked
off the split-screen horse races on his Bang & Olufsen
sixty-inch plasma and yanked off his earpiece.

"You winning?" Ty asked.

Frankly, he wouldn't be all that surprised to find
out that his agent was knee-deep in bookies or debt.
He and Jay had never been friends. No one could
argue that Jay was a master at making the deal, and
the money had always been incredible. But although
Ty had never confirmed his suspicions about Jay's
predilections for hookers and drugs, he wondered if
he'd been wise to let someone just this side of legal
represent him for so many years.

Jay tightened his tie and grabbed a folder off his desk.

"Glad you're here. I just got the contracts for Buzzed Cola. Ever wanted to buy a French chateau?"

"That much money, huh?"

Jay smacked his lips. "The royalties are going to be pouring in for years." He was practically dancing at the prospect of closing this deal. And no wonder: Ten percent of ten million was a million. Someone had to pay for Jay's big-screen TVs, prime location in Union Square, and gambling debts.

But he wasn't going to be the one doing it any-more.

Ty flipped through the thick contract Jay handed him. No question, the numbers looked good. But he already had more money than he could spend. Espe-cially since a *French chateau* wasn't on his need-to-buy list.

"You really think this is a good move? Won't a lot of kids be getting wired on this crap?"

Jay snorted. "So what? Trust me on this, it's a hot product and you're perfect for it."

"I hear what you're saying. There's only one problem."

Panic lit Jay's eyes. "Nothing that can't be solved. You just let me know what you want changed and I'll take care of it."

Ty stood up, picking up the contract to ensure it got disposed of properly. "We've had some good years, Jay, but it's time for me to take my business elsewhere."

Jay scowled. "You would have been nothing without me, you little trailer park punk."

Ty headed for the door feeling like a weight had been lifted from his shoulders. "Maybe, maybe not." The next agent he hired was going to be someone he liked hanging out with.

Jay clearly couldn't resist a parting shot. "You should be thanking me for hooking you up with that fuck-bunny. I bet her pussy was nice and tight and wet."

Ty dropped his hand from the silver doorknob. He was this close to doing a diving leap onto his ex-agent and crushing his skull with a few quick hits.

He nailed Jay with his gaze. "Say whatever you want about me—I don't give a shit. But if anyone even hints that you've said something about Julie, you'd better think about installing an impenetrable security system at your house. And never going outside again."

Ty left the building and jammed a baseball cap onto his head on the sidewalk. What had Jay meant by "You have me to thank"? Hadn't hiring an image consultant been Bobby's idea? At the time, Ty hadn't thought too hard about how quickly Jay had agreed to Bobby's demands. Maybe he should have.

Something was definitely up. But before he figured out what it was, he had a favor to call in.

Pulling out his cell phone, he dialed the NFL headquarters. "Steve, it's Ty Calhoun."

Steve Villers, the vice president of press relations, was a good friend of his, back from his rookie year in Pittsburgh. Steve had retired from the game a couple of years after Ty went pro and had been working for the NFL ever since.

"Dude, your ears must have been burning."

Any other time, Ty would have assumed good things were being said. At present, he'd rather not hear the word on the street.

"I've got a favor to ask you, Steve."

"Always happy to help out a friend."

"I don't know if you heard, but I've been working with an image consultant. A great image consultant. Julie Spencer."

Saying her name aloud brought everything back in a rush. The way she smelled. The taste of her lips. Her curves soft and yielding beneath him.

Steve chuckled. "Trust me, the situation would have been impossible to miss."

Ty got straight to the point. "I think she's been a huge asset to the NFL." He wasn't even sure that Julie would appreciate him putting in a good word for her with the league, but he was willing to try anything at this point.

Besides, if she got this gig then at least he knew he'd see her every once in while. She'd probably act like he was dead, but he'd just keep working on her until she folded under the pressure and gave him another chance.

"No shit," came Steve's reply. "After we saw how good she made a fuck-up like you look, we knew we needed her. She's thinking over our offer."

What an ass he was. Of course the League had noticed what an incredible job Julie had done manipulating—and fixing—his image.

"How about you do *me* a favor?" Steve said, and Ty knew exactly what was coming.

"Don't worry. I'm not going to screw things up for you by telling her I think it's a good idea."

"Are you kidding? She spoke so highly of you, I was going to ask you to put in a good word for us."

Ty nearly blurted, *"She spoke highly of me?"* but it sounded too pathetic, even inside his own head.

Instead he said, "Sure thing, Steve."

He'd never escaped that night with Julie on the boat, not in ten long years of beautiful women. Too bad he'd been an eighteen-year-old chicken-shit weasel, scared by the thought of her dumping his ass because he was just a poor jock. He'd never even tried to make her understand how intensely he felt about her. He'd thought it was easier to let her walk away.

He couldn't have been more wrong.

The next time he saw Julie, he was going to risk his heart, even though he knew the likelihood of getting it crushed was damn high.

CHAPTER THIRTY

Julie stood in the back of the NFL pressroom, more nervous than she'd ever been in all her life. When she thought about what she was about to do, she had to fight the urge to run fast and far.

Oddly, even though she hadn't known the first thing about football just weeks ago, she wasn't nervous about fielding questions about her new role. Since she'd signed on as a League-wide image consultant two days ago, she'd done her homework with how-to videos and a stack of game tapes and interviews with the best players in the game. Of course Ty was among them. No one had to know that she'd watched his segments over and over.

All she wanted was a fresh start: just the two of them, and a little bit of trust that hopefully would blossom into a strong and lasting love.

She scanned the room for the hundredth time.

Why wasn't Ty here yet? What if something had happened to him? What if he was lying in a hospital somewhere? Would he think to call her?

Steve Villers pulled out a chair beside him and Julie tried to focus on the welcome speech the NFL's commissioner was giving, even though all she could think about was seeing Ty again.

The commissioner opened the floor for questions and she wasn't surprised that Bobby Wilson was the first to stand.

"As I'm sure everyone here already knows, I am the new owner of the Outlaws." He smacked his lips together, looking like a hungry wolf on a three-little-pig hunt. "I've got a question for Miss Spencer, if y'all don't mind."

Sensing something juicy, the reporters turned their tape recorders his way.

"First off all, may I say that you are looking just as pretty as ever, Ms. Spencer."

Julie waited for him to get to the point.

"I was wondering about something you said to me in my office a few days back." He paused, pushed his cowboy hat an inch to the left. "If I recall correctly, you said you didn't have the necessary skills to fix up an athlete's public image. I do believe that was right before you told me you were not going to work with my boy Ty any longer."

Just then Ty emerged from a dark corner, looking like he didn't have a care in the world, the way he always did. He raised an eyebrow at her in his cocky way.

God, she loved him. Every arrogant, gorgeous inch of him.

"Something I learned recently is that we all make mistakes. Even an image consultant screws up from time to time." She grinned. "I have a feeling that this will come in very handy in working with professional football players."

Laughter rolled through the crowd and she hoped Ty understood that her words were meant for him.

"Two weeks ago I knew nothing about football. Like a lot of people, I assumed football players were overpaid, dumb jocks."

The players groaned.

"Sorry, guys," she said. "But that's why I've decided to work with the NFL. I've learned a lot about football players: I learned about their integrity and giving, and what's really beneath the surface. The NFL is now my firm's biggest client, and I will devote the bulk of my time and energy to making sure people view both the league and its players in the most positive light imaginable."

She looked straight at Ty. "Misunderstandings will always happen; that's just the way the world works. But from here on out I vow not to let anyone walk away until we've reached a mutual understanding."

Bobby nodded. "A very polished answer, Miss Spencer. There's only one problem with that." He waved a nine-by-twelve manila envelope at her. "I've got pictures of you and Ty Calhoun having sex on a balcony in Napa. How are you going to talk your way out of that one?"

Ty reached Bobby in seconds flat, and yanked the envelope from his hand.

Before Ty could get his hands around Bobby's fleshy neck, a loud crash sounded from the back of the room.

A disheveled, obviously drunk man stumbled into the press conference. "Where is that rat bastard?"

The man wobbled past athletes and writers, finally finding his target in the crowd.

"You lost me my biggest player!" he screamed at Bobby. "Now that he's gone, everyone else is leaving me. I'll have nothing left soon!"

Julie quickly put two and two together. Had Ty fired his smarmy agent?

A plump bead of sweat rolled down Bobby's face.

"I have no idea what you're talking about."

Jay pointed at Bobby with a shaking hand and spittle flew from his lips as he screamed, "You paid me to convince Ty to let some stupid image consultant tail him. You wanted to make Ty look really bad, to get even for what he did to your son."

Ty stood in the middle of the crowded room between his crazy agent and even crazier boss, and his steady voice cut through the shocked silence. "Your son? Have I met him before?" A second later, recognition dawned. "Joey Wilson? From Texas Football Camp? That was your kid?"

"He was going to be a star quarterback," Bobby spat, "until you hogged up all the limelight, you fucking bastard."

"Didn't he want to be a writer or something?"

Bobby's face turned beet red. "He was best in state until you showed up. Then none of the recruiters noticed him—they only had eyes for you, pretty boy. I told my stupid kid that writers don't matter, great football players do. But he wouldn't listen to me. It's all your fault. And your agent was perfectly happy to take my money to make sure you didn't look for another team."

A low growl came from the crowd of journalists. It was one thing to be harsh on an athlete. It was another entirely to have their own profession maligned. Security guards, clearly fearing for Bobby's safety, pushed through the crowd and quickly dragged him out the double doors, squealing the whole way.

*

As the double doors slammed shut Ty shook his head, amazed at how things had gone down. But the whole mess had brought Julie back into his life, and for that reason alone he was willing to forgive anyone anything.

Back behind the podium, the commissioner said, "I apologize for the three-ring-circus that just took place, folks. I think we all need a few minutes to regroup and get some air. Let's start up again at quarter till."

Most of the journalists were already either calling in their stories or typing furiously on their Black-Berries. Ty grinned. He seemed to have a knack for getting press, even when he wasn't trying.

The commissioner approached him first. "I want to personally apologize for what just happened. Bobby Wilson will be suspended and his case reviewed. Let me know if there's anything I can do to make things right."

"Will do." All Ty could concentrate on right now was the woman he loved. He looked through the crowd at where she'd been sitting, but she was gone.

She was standing right in front of him.

"I'm sorry," he said, reaching for her hands, and she said, "No, I am," as she pulled him closer.

"I was an idiot ten years ago," he said. "I figured

you woke up and realized you'd slept with a loser. I thought you were going to leave me." He held her gaze. "So I left you first."

"I've done a lot of stupid things in my life, but not begging you to give me another chance was the stupidest. Until last week, when I let you go again. You're more important to me than any game, than fame or money. I want to share my dreams with you, Julie. You're all I want."

Julie's eyes shone with unshed tears. "I couldn't even be honest about my own life, so how could I be honest about my feelings for you? I shouldn't have insisted on keeping our relationship a secret. I was so scared. But I'm not scared anymore."

Ty took her face in his hands and kissed her softly on the lips.

"I've been running my whole life," she whispered against his mouth. "I don't want to run anymore. I want you, Ty. Your past, your future. Everything." She turned her cheek into his palm and pressed a kiss into it. "I never should have thought you were trying to hurt Jack. You made a difficult choice talking to him. The right choice."

He raised an eyebrow. "Been busy lately, huh?"

"Jack and I had a nice chat. He wants to apologize to you."

"No need."

"I told him that already."

They moved closer to each other in the crowded room, and ten years fell away.

"Do you know what I want to do, Julie?"

She stared at him, holding her breath waiting to hear what he was going to say.

"I want to kiss you. Do you want to kiss me?"

Her voice was full of love when she said, "Yes, I do." She went up on her toes to kiss his lips and slipped her panties into his pants pocket. "I love you, Ty. I always have."

Smiling against her lips, he whispered, "I love you too, Julie. Marry me."

She smiled back. "I'm game for anything. As long as I'm with you."